TELENY

or The Reverse of the Medal

Attributed to

Oscar Wilde

Introduction by Jack Hirschman, Ph.D.

BRANDON BOOKS • CHATSWORTH, CALIFORNIA

Copyright © 1966

by

BRANDON BOOKS
21322 Lassen Street
Chatsworth, California 91311

PRINTED IN THE UNITED STATES OF AMERICA

ISBN 0-87056-261-4

INTRODUCTION

Of *Teleny, or The Reverse of the Medal* it has been said that bookdealers and collectors of erotica have persistently attributed the work to Oscar Wilde. It was published in a strictly limited edition in 1893 (some believe that the date of that first and only edition of the work may be deliberately erroneous, but physical details of the book tend to prove that it actually was printed just before or very soon after that time), the same year that Wilde was refused license in England for his play, *Salome*, which was then printed in France and produced the following year at the Sarah Bernhardt theater. Wilde already was the famous author of *The Picture of Dorian Gray* and the comedy, *Lady Windermere's Fan*. Two years later he was to go on trial, be publicly exposed as a homosexual to a hostile Victorian society and be sentenced to a prison term in what was one of the most incredible scandals in English history.

If Wilde did not author *Teleny* (Victorian

opinion still persists), certainly the writer was more than an expert imitator. For if one looks closely at *The Picture of Dorian Gray*, one will perceive that there is a thematic continuity between that book and *Teleny*, as though the latter were a plunge into the physical confrontations which the former still 'politessed'. Clearly the element of narcissism in *Dorian Gray* is given full embodiment in *Teleny*; there is furthermore a geographical shift to Paris, not insignificant—if one takes students of Wilde seriously—in the sense that it was in that great city that that most flamboyant of dandies could, simply, be accepted. (It should moreover be remembered that after his prison term, Wilde lived on the Continent but, as it were, came to Paris to die, in 1900.)

Paris-London. London-Paris. The story is an old one, not a new one, actually. It is no accident that students of English literature, particularly of Geoffrey Chaucer, are referred to the French work, *The Romance of the Rose*, in order to complete their understanding of England's first great author. Chaucer himself, apart from being in fact a sort of diplomat to France, was in touch with French literature most of his life. Like most English authors he traveled freely on the Continent, for one reason or another (indeed Shakespeare's relative lack of travel marks him as one of the great exceptions in that language), and, reversely speaking, Continental authors often sought asylum in England due to political or civil strife. One thinks of the Italian philosopher and prophet of modern relativity, Giordano Bruno, often called the first modern saint, who was burned at the stake in Italy in 1600 after travels throughout the Continent, including a rich stay in London under the sponsorship of Sir Philip Sydney.

And, more pertinently relative to *Teleny*, one recalls the beautiful prose poem of Stephane Mallarme, called *The Pipe*, written about a refuge that the poet sought, and, for a brief period, achieved in London, away from Parisian life. I mention Mallarme, who was roughly contemporary with Wilde, because the roots of the writing of both these men go back to the work of Charles Baudelaire, rightly called the first modern poet of the Continent. If Baudelaire was the first rich effusion of the flower of voluptuousness which blossomed during the second half of the last century, Mallarme and Wilde represent the paling. But where Mallarme, also a Parisian, developed out of Baudelaire that hermetic perfection of the line that makes most of his work (still) untranslatable, Wilde used his Baudelairesque inheritance to affront an essentially puritanical society, assuming in England Baudelaire's dandyism, shocking the public morals while, at the same time, reporting—by implication— on the colonial and aristocratic breakdown of the English empire. In this sense those who say that Oscar Wilde 'created' the last decade of the last century are quite wrong. As all writers are instruments of their times, as they cannot help but have outstretched those antennae which, in one way or another, pick up the trends and modes of a given epoch, Wilde was in fact reporting on a subterranean arc that bridged life in England and France; and the implications of a work like *Teleny* are as immediately political as they are erotical.

It would be easy, for example, to pass this work off simply as a portrayal of a sodomite civilization, with narcissism at its very root. But then it would be just as easy to say that that is the meaning and message of Proust's *Remembrance of Things Past*. On the contrary, when the narrator of *Teleny* says: "We had once more one body between us, juggling with one another, ever seeking new caresses, new sensations, a sharper and more inebriating kind of lewdness, in our anxiety not only to enjoy ourselves but to make the other one feel"—we are presented with the central theme of all human contact, all human confrontation, and the two beings might just as well be a man and woman, or two women, as, in this case, they are two men. The search for feeling, ultimately for caring to feel, in a world which, at every point, tempts one to its very opposite—to absence of feeling, of caring—is what, simply, has made such a thing as literature happen. The 'new caresses, new sensations' of *Teleny* are objectively of course not new at all, but very old, as old as man himself. But as they appear fresh and new to the actor, and as the actor is here performing in a work of art, they must be acknowledged as being 'new' to him, or at least in search of the novel; and that search is totally involved with a longing to feel, to love. The tragic end of *Teleny* marks another defeat in that search, it is true. But then *Teleny* is not very unlike most literature, with its story of love found and lost, with death and resignation at the end.

In this respect, two other aspects of the book come to mind. The first is its dramatic unfoldment. It is here that those who believe Wilde to be its author are most firmly footed. For the book is a masterful interweaving of novelistic and dramatic elements, and one easily perceives both the prose writer and dramatist at work. Grounded in the *bildungsroman*, or developmental novel, *Teleny* embodies techniques that go back to the beginnings of the form of the novel; for example, the story-within-story form, out of the mannerist novels of the 18th century; and the romantic theme of *sehnsucht*, or longing, which marks off so much literature of Wilde's own century. Dramatically speaking, the book's almost 20th-century use of dialogue is the certain indication that the writer was a man of the theater. And finally, of course, there are those magnificent pastiche touches of insight, mingled at times with a liberal use of the Continental French language, that give the work its admirable stylistic advantage; for example: "He had, however, one great defect—he was an artist, and had an artist's lavishness in the composition of his character. Although he now gained enough to live comfortably, his concerts did not yet afford him the means to live in the princely way he did. I often lectured him on that score; he invariably promised me not to throw away his money, but alas! there was in the web of his nature some of the yarn of which my namesake's mistress—Manon Lescaut—was made."

The shape and contours of those sentences, the premeditated artificiality, the language constructed as though a translation from, and tribute to, the French—all these indicate a work of savage subtlety, a mingling of high and low, one of the last flowers of an English aristocracy before he turned up, immigrant and transmogrified, in spats, baggy pants, derby and cane, and holey gloves on the American screen.

JACK HIRSCHMAN, Ph.D.
Los Angeles, California,

Tell me your story from its very beginning, Des Grieux, said he, interrupting me; and how you got to be acquainted with him.

—It was at a grand charity concert where he was playing; for though amateur performances are one of the many plagues of modern civilization, still, my mother being one of the lady patronesses, I felt it incumbent to be present.

—But he was not an amateur, was he?

—Oh, no! Still, at that time he was only just beginning to make a name.

—Well, go on.

—He had already seated himself at the piano when I got to my *stalle d'orchestre.* The first thing he played was a favorite *gavotte* of mine —one of those slight, graceful and easy melodies that seem to smell of *lavande ambrée,* and in some way or other put you in mind of Lulli and Watteau, of powdered ladies dressed in yellow satin gowns, flirting with their fans.

—And then?

—As he reached the end of the piece, he cast several sidelong glances towards—as I thought —the lady patroness. When he was about to rise, my mother—who was seated behind me— tapped me on my shoulder with her fan, only to make one of the many unseasonable remarks women are forever pestering you with, so that, by the time I had turned round to applaud, he had disappeared.

—And what happened afterwards?

—Let me see. I think there was some singing.

—But did he not play any more?

—Oh, yes! He came out again towards the middle of the concert. As he bowed, before taking his place at the piano, his eyes seemed to be looking out for someone in the pit. It was then—as I thought—that our glances met for the first time.

—What kind of a man was he?

—He was a rather tall and slight young man of twenty-four. His hair, short and curled— after the fashion Bressan, the actor, had brought into vogue—was of a peculiar ashy hue; but this—as I knew afterwards—was due to its being always imperceptibly powdered. Anyhow, the fairness of his hair contrasted with his dark eyebrows and his short moustache. His complexion was of that warm, healthy paleness which, I believe, artists often have in their youth. His eyes—though generally taken for black—were of a deep blue color; and although they appeared so quiet and serene, still, a close observer would every now and then have seen in them a scared and wistful look, as if he were gazing at some dreadful dim and distant vision. An expression of the deepest sorrow invariably succeeded this painful glamour.

—And what was the reason of his sadness?

—At first, whenever I asked him, he always shrugged his shoulders, and answered laughingly, 'Do you never see ghosts?' When I got to be on more intimate terms with him, his invariable reply was—'My fate; that horrible, horrible fate of mine!' But then, smiling and arching his eyebrows, he always hummed, *'Non ci pensiam.'*

—He was not of a gloomy or brooding disposition, was he?

—No, not at all; he was only very superstitious.

—As are all artists, I believe.

—Or rather, all persons like—well, like ourselves; for nothing renders people so superstitious as vice—

—Or ignorance.

—Oh! that is quite a different kind of superstition.

—Was there any peculiar dynamic quality in his eyes?

—For myself of course there was: yet he had not what you would call hypnotizing eyes; his glances were far more dreamy than piercing, or staring; and still they had such penetrating power that, from the very first time I saw him, I felt that he could dive deep into my heart; and although his expression was anything but sensual, still, every time he looked at me, I felt all the blood within my veins was set aglow.

—I have often been told that he was very handsome; is it true?

—Yes, he was remarkably good looking, and still, even more peculiar, than strikingly handsome. His dress, moreover, though always faultless, was a trifle eccentric. That evening, for instance, he wore at his buttonhole a bunch of white heliotrope, although camellias and gardenias were then in fashion. His bearing was most gentlemanly, but on the stage—as well as with strangers—slightly supercilious.

—Well, after your glances met?

—He sat down and began to play. I looked at the program; it was a wild Hungarian rhapsody by an unknown composer with a crackjaw name; its effect, however, was perfectly entrancing. In fact, in no music is the sensuous element so powerful as in that of the Tsiganes. You see, from a minor scale—

—Oh! please no technical terms, for I hardly know one note from another.

—Anyhow, if you have ever heard a tsardas,

you must have felt that, although the Hungarian music is replete with rare rhythmical effects, still, as it quite differs from our set rules of harmony, it jars upon our ears. These melodies begin by shocking us, then by degrees subdue, until at last they enthrall us. The gorgeous fioriture, for instance, with which they abound are of decided luxurious Arabic character, and—

—Well, never mind about the fioriture of the Hungarian music, and do go on with your story.

—That is just the difficult point, for you cannot disconnect him from the music of his country; nay, to understand him you must begin by feeling the latent spell which pervades every song of Tsigane. A nervous organization —having once been impressed by the charm of a tsardas—ever thrills in response to those magic numbers. Those strains usually begin with a soft and low andante, something like the plaintive wail of forlorn hope, then the ever changing rhythm—increasing in swiftness—becomes 'wild as the accents of lovers' farewell,' and without losing any of its sweetness, but always acquiring new vigor and solemnity, the prestissimo—syncopated by sighs—reaches a paroxysm of mysterious passion, now melting into a mournful dirge, then bursting out into the brazen blast of a fiery and warlike anthem.

He, in beauty, as well as in character, was the very personification of this entrancing music.

As I listened to his playing I was spellbound; yet I could hardly tell whether it was with the composition, the execution, or the player himself. At the same time the strangest visions began to float before my eyes. First I saw the Alhambra in all the luxuriant loveliness of its Moorish masonry—those sumptuous symphonies of stones and bricks—so like the flourishes of those quaint gipsy melodies. Then a smouldering unknown fire began to kindle itself within my breast. I longed to feel that mighty love which maddens one to crime, to feel the blasting lust of men who live beneath the scorching sun, to drink down deep from the cup of some satyrion philter.

The vision changed; instead of Spain, I saw a barren land, the sun-lit sands of Egypt, wet by the sluggish Nile; where Adrian stood wailing, forlorn, disconsolate for he had lost forever the lad he loved so well. Spellbound by that soft music, which sharpened every sense, I now began to understand things hitherto so strange, the love the mighty monarch felt for his fair Grecian slave, Antinous, who—like unto Christ —died for his master's sake. And thereupon my blood all rushed from my heart into my head, then it coursed down, through every vein, like waves of molten lead.

The scene then changed, and shifted into the gorgeous towns of Sodom and Gomorrah, weird, beautiful and grand; to me the pianist's notes just then seemed murmuring in my ear with the panting of an eager lust, the sound of thrilling kisses.

Then—in the very midst of my vision—the pianist turned his head and cast one long, lingering, slumberous look at me, and our glances met again. But was he the pianist, was he Antinous, or rather, was he not one of those two angels which God sent to Lot? Anyhow, the irresistible charm of his beauty was such that I was quite overcome by it; and the music just then seemed to whisper:

> *Could you not drink his gaze like wine,*
> *Yet though its splendour swoon*
> *In the silence languidly*
> *As a tune into a tune?*

That thrilling longing I had felt grew more and more intense, the craving so insatiable that it was changed to pain; the burning fire had now been fanned into a mighty flame, and my whole body was convulsed and wracked with mad desire. My lips were parched, I gasped for breath; my joints were stiff, my veins were swollen, yet I sat still, like all the crowd around me. But suddenly a heavy hand seemed to be laid upon my lap, something was bent and clasped and grasped, which made me faint with lust. The hand moved up and down, slowly at first, then fast and faster it went in rhythm with the song. My brain began to reel as throughout every vein a burning lava coursed, and then, some drops even gushed out — I panted —

All at once the pianist finished his piece with a crash amidst the thundering applause of the whole theatre. I myself heard nothing but the din of thunder, I saw a fiery hail, a rain of rubies and emeralds that was consuming the cities of the plain, and he, the pianist, standing naked in the lurid light, exposing himself to the thunderbolts of heaven and to the flames of hell. As he stood there, I saw him—in my madness—change all at once into Anubis, the dog-headed God of Egypt, then by degrees into a loathsome poodle. I started, I shivered, felt sick, but speedily he changed to his own form again.

I was powerless to applaud; I sat there dumb, motionless, nerveless, exhausted. My eyes were fixed upon the artist who stood there bowing listlessly, scornfully; while his own glances full of 'eag___ 1 impassioned tenderness,' seemed to be seeking mine and mine alone. What a feeling of exultation awakened within me! But could he love me, and me only? For a moment the exultation gave way to bitter jealousy. Was I growing mad, I asked myself?

As I looked at him, his features seemed to be overshadowed by a deep melancholy, and—horrible to behold—I saw a small dagger plunged in his breast, with the blood flowing fast from the wound. I not only shuddered, but almost shrieked with fear, the vision was so real. My head was spinning round, I was growing faint and sick, I fell back exhausted in my chair, covering my eyes with my hands.

—What a strange hallucination, I wonder what brought it about?

—It was, indeed, something more than an hallucination, as you will see hereafter. When I lifted up my head again, the pianist was gone. I then turned round, and my mother—seeing how pale I was—asked me if I felt ill. I muttered something about the heat being very oppressive.

'Go into the green room,' said she, 'and have a glass of water.'

'No, I think I had better go home.'

I felt, in fact, that I could not listen to any more music that evening. My nerves were so utterly unstrung that a maudlin song would just then have exasperated me, while another intoxicating melody might have made me lose my senses.

As I got up I felt so weak and exhausted that it seemed as if I were walking in a trance, so, without exactly knowing whither I wended my steps, I mechanically followed some persons in front of me, and, a few moments afterwards, I unexpectedly found myself in the green room.

The salon was almost empty. At the further end a few dandies were grouped around a young man in evening dress, whose back was turned towards me. I recognized one of them as Briancourt.

—What, the General's son?

—Precisely.

—I remember him. He always dressed in such a conspicuous way.

—Quite so. That evening, for instance, when every gentleman was in black, he, on the contrary, wore a white flannel suit, as usual, a very open Byron-like collar, and a red Lavallière cravat tied in a huge bow.

—Yes, for he had a most lovely neck and throat.

—He was very handsome, although I, for myself, had always tried to avoid him. He had a way of ogling which made me feel quite uncomfortable. You laugh, but it is quite true. There are some men who, when staring at a woman, seem all the while to be undressing her. Briancourt had that indecent way of looking at everybody. I vaguely felt his eyes all over me, and that made me shudder.

—But you were acquainted with him, were you not?

—Yes, we had been at some Kindergarten or other together, but, being three years younger than he, I was always in a lower class. Anyhow, that evening, upon perceiving him, I was about to leave the room, when the gentleman in the evening suit turned round. It was the pianist. As our eyes met again, I felt a strange flutter within me, and the fascination of his looks was so powerful that I was hardly able to move. Then, attracted onwards as I was, instead of quitting the green room, I walked on slowly, almost reluctantly, toward the group. The musician, without staring, did not, how-

10

ever, turn his eyes away from me. I was quivering from head to foot. He seemed to be slowly drawing me to him, and I must confess the feeling was such a pleasant one that I yielded entirely to it.

Just then Briancourt, who had not seen me, turned round, and recognizing me, nodded in his off-hand way. As he did so, the pianist's eyes brightened, and he whispered something to him, whereupon the General's son, without giving him any answer, turned towards me, and, taking me by the hand, said:

'Camille, allow me to introduce you to my friend René. M. René Teleny—M. Camille Des Grieux.'

I bowed, blushing. The pianist stretched forth his ungloved hand. In my fit of nervousness I had pulled off both my gloves, so that I now put my bare hand into his.

He had a perfect hand for a man, rather large than small, strong yet soft, and with long, tapering fingers, so that his grasp was firm and steady.

Who has not been sentient of the manifold feelings produced by the touch of a hand? Many persons seem to bear a temperature of their own about them. They are hot and feverish in mid-winter, while others are cold and icy in the dog-days. Some hands are dry and parched, others continually moist, clammy, and slimy. There are fleshy, pulpy, muscular, or thin, skeletal and bony hands. The grasp of some is like that of an iron vise, others feel as limp as a bit of rag. There is the artificial product of our modern civilization, a deformity like a Chinese lady's foot, always enclosed in a glove during the day, often poulticed at night, tended by a manicure; they are as white as snow, if not as chaste as ice. How that little useless hand would shrink from the touch of the gaunt, horny, clay-colored, begrimed workman's hand, which hard, unremitting labor has changed into a kind of hoof. Some hands are coy, others paddle you indecently; the grip of some is hypocritical, and not what it pretends to be; there is the velvety, the unctuous, the priestly, the humbug's hand; the open palm of the spendthrift, the usurer's tight-fisted claw. There is, moreover, the magnetic hand, which seems to have a secret affinity for your own; its simple touch thrills your whole nervous system, and fills you with delight.

How can I express all that I felt from the contact of Teleny's hand? It set me on fire; and, strange to say, it soothed me at the same time. How much sweeter, softer, it was, than any woman's kiss. I felt his grasp steal slowly over all my body, caressing my lips, my throat, my breast; my nerves quivered from head to foot with delight, then it sank downwards into my veins, and Priapus, reawakened, lifted up his head. I actually felt I was being taken possession of, and I was happy to belong to him.

I should have liked to have said something polite in acknowledgment of the pleasure he had given me by his playing, still, what unhackneyed phrase could have expressed all the admiration I felt for him?

'But, gentlemen,' said he, 'I am afraid I am keeping you away from the music.'

'I, myself, was just going away,' said I.

'The concert bores you then, does it?'

'No, on the contrary; but after having heard you play, I cannot listen to any more music tonight.'

He smiled and looked pleased.

'In fact, René, you have outdone yourself this evening,' said Briancourt. 'I never heard you play like that before.'

'Do you know why?'

'No, unless it is that you had such a full theatre.'

'Oh, no! it is simply because, while I was playing the gavotte, I felt that somebody was listening to me.'

'Oh! somebody!' echoed the young men, laughing.

'Amongst a French public, especially that of a charity concert, do you really think that there are many persons who listen? I mean who listen intently with all their heart and soul. The young men are obliging the ladies, these are scrutinizing each other's toilette; the fathers, who are bored, are either thinking of the rise and fall of the stocks, or else counting the number of gaslights, and reckoning how much the illumination will cost.'

'Still, among such a crowd there is surely

more than one attentive listener,' said Odillot, the lawyer.

'Oh, yes! I dare say; as for instance the young lady who has been thrumming the piece you have just played, but there is hardly more than one—how can I express it?—well, more than one sympathetic listener.'

'What do you mean by a sympathetic listener?' asked Courtois, the stockbroker.

'A person with whom a current seems to establish itself; someone who feels, while listening, exactly as I do while I am playing, who sees perhaps the same visions as I do—'

'What! do you see visions when you play?' asked one of the bystanders, astonished.

'Not as a rule, but always when I have a sympathetic listener.'

'And do you often have such a listener?' said I, with a sharp pang of jealousy.

'Often? Oh, no! seldom, very seldom, hardly ever in fact, and then—'

'Then what?'

'Never like the one of this evening.'

'And when you have no listener?' asked Courtois.

'Then I play mechanically, and in a humdrum kind of way.'

'Can you guess whom your listener was this evening?' added Briancourt, smiling sardonically, and then with a leer at me.

'One of the many beautiful ladies of course,' sighed Odillot, 'you are a lucky fellow.'

'Yes,' said another, 'I wish I were your neighbor at that table d'hote, so you might pass me the dish after you have helped yourself.'

'Was it some beautiful girl?' said Courtois questioningly. Teleny looked deeply into my eyes, smiled faintly, and replied:

'Perhaps.'

'Do you think you will ever know your listener?' enquired Briancourt.

Teleny again fixed his eyes on mine, and added faintly:

'Perhaps.'

'But what clue have you to lead to this discovery?' asked Odillot.

'His visions must coincide with mine.'

'I know what my vision would be if I had any,' said Odillot.

'What would it be?' enquired Courtois.

'Two lily-white breasts with nipples like two pink rosebuds, and lower down, two moist lips like those pink shells which, opening with awakening lust, reveal a pulpy, luxurious world, only of a deep coralline hue, and then these two pouting lips must be surrounded by a slight golden or black down—'

'Enough, enough, Odillot, my mouth waters at your vision, and my tongue longs to taste the flavor of those lips,' said the stockbroker, his eyes gleaming like those of a satyr, and evidently in a state of priapism.

'Is that not your vision, Teleny?'

The pianist smiled enigmatically:

'Perhaps.'

'As for me,' said one of the young men who

had not yet spoken, 'a vision evoked by a Hungarian rhapsody would be either of vast plains, of bands of gipsies, or of men with round hats, wide trousers and short jackets, riding on fiery horses.'

'Or of booted and laced soldiers dancing with black-eyed girls,' added another.

I smiled, thinking how different my vision had been from these. Teleny, who was watching me, noticed the movement of my lips.

'Gentlemen,' said the musician, 'Odillot's vision was provoked not by my playing, but by some good-looking young girl he had been ogling; as for yours, they are simply reminiscences of some pictures or ballet.'

'What was your vision, then?' asked Briancourt.

'I was just going to put you the same question,' retorted the pianist.

'My vision was something like Odillot's though not exactly the same.'

'Then it must have been *le revers de la médaille*—the back side,' quoth the lawyer, laughing; 'that is, two snow-clad lovely hillocks and deep in the valley below, a well, a tiny hole with a dark margin, or rather a brown halo around it.'

'Well, let us have your vision now,' insisted Briancourt.

'My visions are so vague and indistinct, they fade away so quickly, that I can hardly remember them,' he answered evasively.

'But they are beautiful, are they not?'

'And horrible withal,' he said enigmatically.

'Like the god-like corpse of Antinous, seen by the silvery light of the opaline moon, floating on the lurid waters of the Nile,' I said.

All the young men looked astonished at me. Briancourt laughed in a jarring way.

'You are a poet or a painter,' said Teleny, gazing at me with half-shut eyes. Then, after a pause: 'Anyhow, you are right to quiz me, but you must not mind my visionary speeches, for there is always so much of the madman in the composition of every artist.' Then, darting a dim ray from his sad eyes deep into mine, 'When you are better acquainted with me, you will know that there is so much more of the madman than of the artist in me.'

Thereupon he took out a strongly-scented fine lawn handkerchief, and wiped the perspiration from his forehead.

'And now,' he added, 'I must not keep you here a minute longer with my idle talk, otherwise the lady patroness will be angry, and I really cannot afford to displease the ladies,' and with a stealthy glance at Briancourt, 'Can I?' he added.

'No, that would be a crime against the fair sex,' replied one.

'Moreover, the other musicians would say I did it out of spite; for no one is gifted with such strong feelings of jealousy as amateurs, be they actors, singers, or instrumentalists, so *au revoir*.'

Then, with a deeper bow than he had vouchsafed to the public, he was about to leave the room, when he stopped again: 'But you, M. Des Grieux, you said you were not going to stay, may I request the pleasure of your company?'

'Most willingly,' said I, eagerly.

Briancourt again smiled ironically—why, I could not understand. Then he hummed a snatch of 'Madame Angot,' which operette was then in fashion, the only words which caught my ears being—

Il est, dit-on, le favori,

and these were marked purposely.

Teleny, who had heard them as well as I had, shrugged his shoulders, and muttered something between his teeth.

'A carriage is waiting for me at the back door,' said he, slipping his arm under mine. 'Still, if you prefer walking—'

'Very much so, for it has been so stiflingly hot in the theatre.'

'Yes, very hot,' he added, repeating my words, and evidently thinking of something else. Then all at once, as if struck by a sudden thought, 'Are you superstitious?' said he.

'Superstitious?' I was struck by the quaintness of his question. 'Well—yes, rather, I believe.'

'I am very much so. I suppose it is my nature, for you see the gipsy element is strong in me. They say that educated people are not superstitious. Well, first I have had a wretched education; and then I think that if we really knew the mysteries of nature, we could probably explain all those strange coincidences that are ever happening.' Then, stopping abruptly, 'Do you believe in the transmission of thought, of sensations?'

'Well, I really do not know—I—'

'You must believe,' he added authoritatively. 'You see we have had the same vision at once. The first thing you saw was the Alhambra, blazing in the fiery light of the sun, was it not?'

'It was,' said I, astonished.

'And you thought you would like to feel that powerful withering love that shatters both the body and the soul? You do not answer. Then afterwards came Egypt, Antinous and Adrian. You were the Emperor, I was the slave.'

Then, musingly, he added, almost to himself: 'Who knows, perhaps I shall die for you one day!' And his features assumed that sweet resigned look which is seen on the demi-god's statues.

I looked at him, bewildered.

'Oh! you think I am mad, but I am not, I am only stating facts. You did not feel that you were Adrian, simply because you are not accustomed to such visions; doubtless all this will be clearer to you someday; as for me, there is, you must know, Asiatic blood in my veins, and—'

But he did not finish his phrase, and we walked on for a while in silence, then:

'Did you not see me turn round during the gavotte, and look for you? I began to feel you just then, but I could not find you out; you remember, don't you?'

'Yes, I did see you look towards my side, and—'

'And you were jealous!'

'Yes,' said I, almost inaudibly.

He pressed my arm strongly against his body for all answer, then after a pause, he added hurriedly, and in a whisper:

'You must know that I do not care for a single girl in this world, I never did, I could never love a woman.'

My heart was beating strongly; I felt a choking feeling as if something was gripping my throat.

'Why should he be telling me this?' said I to myself.

'Did you not smell a scent just then?'

'A scent—when?'

'When I was playing the gavotte; you have forgotten perhaps.'

'Let me see, you are right, what scent was it?'

'*Lavande ambrée.*'

'Exactly.'

'Which you do not care for, and which I dislike; tell me, which is your favorite scent?'

'*Heliotrope blanc.*'

Without giving me an answer, he pulled out his handkerchief and gave it to me to smell.

'All our tastes are exactly the same, are they not?' And saying this, he looked at me with such a passionate and voluptuous longing, that the carnal hunger depicted in his eyes made me feel faint.

'You see, I always wear a bunch of white heliotrope; let me give this to you, that its smell may remind you of me tonight, and perhaps make you dream of me.'

And taking the flowers from his buttonhole, he put them into mine with one hand, whilst he slipped his left arm round my waist and clasped me tightly, pressing me against his whole body for a few seconds. That short space of time seemed to me an eternity.

I could feel his hot and panting breath against my lips. Below, our knees touched, and I felt something hard press and move against my thigh.

My emotion just then was such that I could hardly stand; for a moment I thought he would kiss me—nay, the crisp hair of his moustache was slightly tickling my lips, producing a most delightful sensation. However, he only looked deep into my eyes with a demoniac fascination.

I felt the fire of his glances sink deep into my breast, and far below. My blood began to boil and bubble like a burning fluid, so that I felt my (what the Italians call a 'birdie,' and what they have portrayed as a winged cherub) struggle within its prison, lift up its head, open its tiny lips, and again spout one or two drops of that creamy, life-giving fluid.

But those few tears—far from being a soothing balm—seemed to be drops of caustic, burning me, and producing a strong, unbearable irritation.

I was tortured. My mind was a hell. My body was on fire.

'Is he suffering as much as I am?' said I to myself.

Just then he unclasped his arm from round my waist, and it fell lifeless of its own weight like that of a man asleep.

He stepped back, and shuddered as if he had received a strong electric shock. He seemed faint for a moment, then wiped his damp forehead, and sighed loudly. All the color had fled from his face, and he became deathly pale.

'Do you think me mad?' said he. Then, without waiting for a reply: 'But who is sane and who is mad? Who is virtuous and who is vicious in this world of ours? Do you know? I don't.'

The thought of my father came to my mind, and I asked myself, shuddering, whether my senses, too, were leaving me.

There was a pause. Neither of us spoke for some time. He had entwined his fingers within mine, and we walked on for a while in silence.

All the blood vessels of my member were still strongly extended and the nerves stiff, the spermatic ducts full to overflowing; therefore, the erection continuing, I felt a dull pain spread over and near all the organs of generation, whilst the remainder of my body was in a state of prostration, and still—notwithstanding the pain and languor—it was a most pleasurable feeling to walk on quietly with our hands clasped, his head almost leaning on my shoulder.

'When did you first feel my eyes on yours?' he asked in a low hushed tone, after some time.

'When you came out for the second time.'

'Exactly; then our glances met, and then there was a current between us, like a spark of electricity running along a wire, was it not?'

'Yes, an uninterrupted current.'

'But you really felt me just before I went out, is it not true?'

For all answer I pressed his fingers tightly.

I finally came to my senses. Being now thoroughly awake, my mother made me understand that hearing me groan and shriek, she had come in to see if I were unwell. Of course I hastened to assure her that I was in perfect health, and had only been the prey of a frightful nightmare. She thereupon put her fresh hand upon my hot forehead. The soothing touch of her soft hand cooled the fire burning within my brain, and allayed the fever raging in my blood.

When I was quietened, she made me drink a

bumper of sugared water flavored with essence of orange-flowers, and then left me. I once more dropped off to sleep. I awoke, however, several times, and always to see the pianist before me.

On the morrow likewise, when I came to myself, his name was ringing in my ears, my lips were muttering it, and my first thoughts reverted to him. I saw him—in my mind's eye—standing there on the stage, bowing before the public, his burning glances rivetted on mine.

I lay for some time in my bed, drowsily contemplating that sweet vision, so vague and indefinite, trying to recall his features which had got mixed up with those of the several statues of Antinous which I had seen.

Analyzing my feelings, I was now conscious that a new sensation had come over me — a vague feeling of uneasiness and unrest. There was an emptiness in me, still I could not understand if the void was in my heart or in my head. I had lost nothing and yet I felt lonely, forlorn, nay almost bereaved. I tried to fathom my morbid state, and all I could find out was that my feelings were akin to those of being homesick or mothersick, with this simple difference, that the exile knows what his cravings are, but I did not. It was something indefinite like the *Sehnsucht* of which the Germans speak so much, and which they really feel so little.

The image of Teleny haunted me, the name of René was ever on my lips. I kept repeating it over and over for dozens of times. What a sweet name it was! At its sound my heart was beating faster. My blood seemed to have become warmer and thicker. I got up slowly. I loitered over my dress. I stared at myself within the looking glass, and I saw Teleny in it instead of myself; and behind him rose our blended shadows, as I had seen them on the pavement the evening before.

Presently the servant tapped at the door; this recalled me to self-consciousness. I saw myself in the glass, and found myself hideous, and for the first time in my life I wished myself good-looking—nay, entrancingly handsome.

The servant who had knocked at the door informed me that my mother was in the breakfast-room, and had sent to see if I were unwell. The name of my mother recalled my dream to my mind, and for the first time I almost preferred not meeting her.

—Still, you were then on good terms with your mother, were you not?

—Certainly. Whatever faults she might have had, no one could have been more affectionate; and though she was said to be somewhat light and fond of pleasure, she had never neglected me.

—She struck me, indeed, as a talented person, when I knew her.

—Quite so; in other circumstances she might have proved even a superior woman. Very orderly and practical in all her household arrangements, she always found plenty of time for everything. If her life was not according to what we generally call 'the principles of morality,' or rather, Christian hypocrisy, the fault was my father's, not hers, as I shall perhaps tell you some other time.

As I entered the breakfast-room, my mother was struck with the change in my appearance, and she asked me if I was feeling unwell.

'I must have a little fever,' I replied; 'besides, the weather is so sultry and oppressive.'

'Oppressive?' quoth she, smiling.

'Is it not?'

'No; on the contrary, it is quite bracing. See, the barometer has risen considerably.'

'Well, then, it must have been your concert that upset my nerves.'

'My concert!' said my mother, smiling, and handing me some coffee.

It was useless for me to try to taste it, the very sight of it turned me sick.

My mother looked at me rather anxiously.

'It is nothing, only for some time back I have been getting sick of coffee.'

'Sick of coffee? You never said so before.'

'Did I not?' I said absently.

'Will you have some chocolate, or some tea?'

'Can I not fast for once?'

'Yes, if you are ill—or if you have some great sin to atone for.'

I looked at her and shuddered. Could she be reading my thoughts better than myself?

'A sin?' quoth I, with an astonished look.

'Well, you know even the righteous—'

'And what then?' I said, interrupting her

snappishly; but to make up for my supercilious way of speaking, I added in gentler tones:

'I do not feel hungry; still, to please you, I'll have a glass of champagne and a biscuit.'

'Champagne, did you say?'

'Yes.'

'So early in the morning, and on an empty stomach?'

'Well, then I'll have nothing at all,' I answered pettishly. 'I see you are afraid I'm going to turn drunkard.'

My mother said nothing, she only looked at me wistfully for a few minutes, an expression of deep sorrow was seen in her face, then — without adding another word — she rang the bell and ordered the wine to be brought.

—But what made her so sad?

—Later on, I understood that she was frightened that I was already getting to be like my father.

—And your father—?

—I'll tell you his story another time.

After I had gulped down a glass or two of champagne, I felt revived by the exhilarating wine; our conversation then turned on the concert, and although I longed to ask my mother if she knew anything about Teleny, still I durst not utter the name which was foremost on my lips, nay I had even to restrain myself not to repeat it aloud every now and then.

At last my mother spoke of him herself, commending first his playing and then his beauty.

'What, do you find him good-looking?' I asked abruptly.

'I should think so,' she replied, arching her eyebrows in an astonished way, 'is there anybody who does not? Every woman finds him an Adonis; but then you men differ so much from us in your admiration for your own sex, that you sometimes find insipid those whom we are taken up with. Anyhow, he is sure to succeed as an artist, as all the ladies will be falling in love with him.'

I tried not to wince upon hearing these last words, but do what I could, it was impossible to keep my features quite motionless.

My mother, seeing me frown, added, smilingly:

'What, Camille, are you going to become as vain as some acknowledged belle, who cannot hear anybody made much of without feeling that any praise given to another woman is so much subtracted from what is due to her?'

'All women are free to fall in love with him if they choose,' I answered snappishly, 'you know quite well that I never piqued myself either on my good looks or upon my conquests.'

'No, it is true, still, today you are like the dog in the manger, for what is it to you whether the women are taken up with him or not, especially if it is such a help to him in his career?'

'But cannot an artist rise to eminence by his talent alone?'

'Sometimes,' she added with an incredulous

smile, 'though seldom, and only with that super-human perseverance which gifted persons often lack, and Teleny—'

My mother did not finish her phrase in words, but the expression of her face, and above all of the corners of her mouth, revealed her thoughts.

'And you think that this young man is such a degraded being as to allow himself to be kept by a woman, like a—'

'Well, it is not exactly being kept—at least, he would not consider it in that light. He might, moreover, allow himself to be helped in a thousand ways other than by money, but his piano would be his *gagnepain*.'

'Just like the stage is for most ballet-girls; then I should not like to be an artist.'

'Oh! they are not the only men who owe their success to a mistress, or to a wife. Read "Bel Ami," and you will see that many a successful man, and even more than one celebrated personage, owes his greatness to—'

'A woman?'

'Exactly; it is always: *Cherchez la femme.*'

'Then this is a disgusting world.'

'Having to live in it, we must take the best of it we can, and not take matters quite so tragically as you do.'

'Anyhow, he plays well. In fact, I never heard anyone play like he did last night.'

'Yes, I grant that last night he did play brilliantly, or, rather, sensationally; but it also must be admitted that you were in a rather morbid state of health and mind, so that music must have had an uncommon effect upon your nerves.'

'Oh! you think there was an evil spirit within me troubling me, and that a cunning player—as the Bible has it—was alone able to quiet my nerves.'

My mother smiled.

'Well, nowadays, we are all of us more or less like Saul; that is to say, we are all occasionally troubled with an evil spirit.'

Thereupon her brow grew clouded, and she interrupted herself, for evidently the remembrance of my late father came to her mind; then she added, musingly—

'And Saul was really to be pitied.'

I did not give her an answer. I was only thinking why David had found favor in Saul's sight. Was it because 'he was ruddy, and withal of a beautiful countenance, and goodly to look to'? Was it also for this reason that, as soon as Jonathan had seen him, 'the soul of Jonathan was knit with the soul of David, and Jonathan loved him as his own soul'?

Was Teleny's soul knit with my own? Was I to love and hate him, as Saul loved and hated David? Anyhow, I despised myself and my folly. I felt a grudge against the musician who had bewitched me; above all, I loathed the whole of womankind, the curse of the world.

All at once my mother drew me from my gloomy thoughts.

'You are not going to the office today, if you do not feel well,' said she, after a while.

—What! you were in trade then, were you?

—Yes, my father had left me a very profitable business, and a most trustworthy and excellent manager who for years had been the soul of the house. I was then twenty-two, and my part in the concern was to pocket the lion's share of the profits. Still, I must say I not only had never been lazy, but, moreover, was rather serious for a young man of my age, and, above all, in my circumstances. I had but one hobby—a most harmless one. I was fond of old majolica, old fans, and old lace, of which I have now a rather fine collection.

—The finest one I ever saw.

—Well, I went to the office as usual, but do what I could it was quite impossible for me to settle down to any kind of work.

Teleny's vision was mixing itself up with whatever I happened to be doing, muddling everything up. Moreover, my mother's words were ever present to my mind. Every woman was in love with him, and their love was necessary to him. I thereupon tried hard to banish him from my thoughts. 'Where there is a will there is a way,' said I to myself, 'so I shall soon get rid of this foolish, maudlin infatuation.'

—But you did not succeed, did you?

—No! the more I tried not to think of him, the more I did think. Have you in fact ever heard some snatches of a half-remembered tune ringing in your ears? Go where you will, listen to whatever you like, that tune is ever tantalizing you. You can no more recollect the whole of it than you can get rid of it. If you go to bed it keeps you from falling asleep; you slumber and you hear it in your dreams; you wake, and it is the very first thing you hear. So it was with Teleny; he actually haunted me, his voice — so sweet and low — was ever repeating in those unknown accents: Oh! friend, my heart doth yearn for thee.

And now his lovely image never left my eyes, the touch of his soft hand was still on mine, I even felt his scented breath upon my lips; thus in that eager longing, every now and then I stretched my arms to seize and to strain him to my breast, and the hallucination was so strong in me that soon I fancied I could feel his body on my own.

A strong erection thereupon took place, which stiffened every nerve and almost made me mad; but though I suffered, still, the pain I felt was sweet.

—Excuse my interrupting you, but had you never been in love before you had met Teleny?

—Never.

—Strange.

—Why so?

—At two-and-twenty?

—Well, you see I was predisposed to love men and not women, and without knowing it I had always struggled against the inclinations of my nature. It is true that several times I thought I had already been in love, still it was only upon knowing Teleny that I understood what real love was. Like all boys I had believed myself bound to feel spoony, and I had done my best to persuade myself that I was deeply smitten. Having once casually come across a young girl with laughing eyes, I had concluded that she was just what an ideal Dulcinea ought to be; I therefore followed her about, every time I met her, and sometimes even tried to think of her at odd moments, when I had nothing to do.

—And how did the affair end?

—In a most ridiculous way. The thing happened, I think, about a year or two before I left the *Lycée;* yes, I remember, it was during the midsummer holidays, and the very first time I had ever travelled alone.

Being of a rather shy disposition, I was somewhat flurried and nervous at having to elbow my way through the crowd, to hurry and push about to get my ticket, to take care so as not to get into a train going in the wrong direction.

The upshot of all this was that, before being thoroughly aware of it, I found myself seated in front of the girl I believed myself in love with, and moreover in a carriage reserved for the fair sex.

Unfortunately, in the same carriage there was a creature who surely could not go under that denomination; for, although I cannot swear as to her sex, I can take my oath she was not fair. In fact, as far as I can remember her, she was a real specimen of the wandering English old maid, clad in a waterproof coat something like an ulster. One of those heterogenous creatures continually met with on the Continent, and I think everywhere else except in England; for I have come to the conclusion that Great Britain manufactures them especially for exportation. Anyhow, I had hardly taken my place, when—

'Monseer,' says she, in a snarling, barking way, 'cette compartement est reserved for dames soules.'

I suppose she meant *'seules,'* but at that moment, confused as I was, I took her at her word.

'Dames soules!' — 'drunken ladies!' said I, terrified, looking around at all the ladies.

My neighbors began to titter.

'Madame says that this carriage is reserved for ladies,' added the mother of my girl, 'of course a young man is not—well, not expected to smoke here, but—'

'Oh! if that is the only objection I certainly shall not allow myself to smoke.'

'No, no!' said the old maid, evidently much shocked, 'vous exit, go out, ou moi crier! Garde,' she shouted out of the window, 'faites go out cette monseer!'

The guard appeared at the door, and not only ordered, but ignominiously turned me out of that carriage, just as if I had been a second Col. Baker.

I was so ashamed of myself, so mortified, that my stomach—which had always been delicate—was actually quite upset by the shock I had received, therefore no sooner had the train started than I began to be, first uncomfortable, then to feel a rumbling pain, and at last a pressing want, so much so that I could hardly sit down on my seat, squeeze as much as I could, and I dared not move for fear of the consequences.

After some time the train stopped for a few minutes, no guard came to open the carriage door, I managed to get up, no guard was to be seen, no place where I could ease myself. I was debating what to do when the train started off.

The only occupant of the carriagè was an old gentleman, who—having told me to make myself comfortable, or rather to put myself at my ease—went off to sleep and snored like a top; I might as well have been alone.

I formed several plans for unburdening my stomach, which was growing more unruly every moment, but only one or two seemed the answer; and yet I could not put them into execution, for my lady-love, only a few carriages off, was every now and then looking out of the window, so it would never have done if, instead of my face, she all at once saw—my full moon. I could not for the same reason use my hat as what the Italians call—a *comodina,* especially as the wind was blowing strongly towards her.

The train stopped again, but only for three minutes. What could one do in three minutes, especially with a stomach-ache like mine? Another stoppage; two minutes. By dint of squeezing I now felt that I could wait a little longer.

The train moved and then once more came to a standstill. Six minutes. Now was my chance, or never. I jumped out.

It was a kind of country station, apparently a junction, and everybody was getting out.

The guard bawled out: '*Les voyageurs pour —en voiture.*'

'Where is the lavatory?' I enquired of him.

He attempted to shove me into the train. I broke loose, and asked the same question of another official.

'There,' said he, pointing to the water-closet, 'but be quick.'

I ran towards it, I rushed into it without looking where I went. I violently pushed open the door.

I heard first a groan of ease and of comfort, followed by a splash and a waterfall, then a screech, and I saw my English damsel, not sitting, but perched upon the closet seat.

The engine whistled, the bell rang, the guard blew his horn, the train was moving.

I ran back as fast as I could, regardless of consequences, holding my falling trousers in my hands, and followed by the wrathful, screeching English old maid, very much like a wee chicken running away from an old hen.

—And—

—Everyone was at the carriage windows laughing at my misadventure.

A few days afterwards I was with my parents at the Pension Bellevue, at the baths of N—, when, on going down to the table d'hote dinner, I was surprised to find the young lady in question seated with her mother, almost opposite to the place usually occupied by my parents. Upon seeing her, I, of course, blushed scarlet, I sat down, and she and the elderly lady exchanged glances and smiled. I wriggled on my chair in a most uncomfortable way, and I dropped the spoon which I had taken up.

'What is the matter with you, Camille?' asked my mother, seeing me grow red and pale.

'Oh, nothing! Only I—I—that is to say, my—my stomach is rather out of order,' said I, in a whisper, finding no better excuse on the spur of the moment.

'Your stomach again?' said my mother, in an undertone.

'What, Camille! have you the belly-ache?' said my father, in his off-hand way, and with his stentorian voice.

I was so ashamed of myself and so upset, that, hungry as I was, my stomach began to make the most fearful rumbling noises.

Everyone at table, I think, was giggling, when all at once I heard a well-known, snarling, barking, shrill voice say—

'Gaason, demandez that monseer not to parler cochonneries at table.'

I cast a glance towards the side whence the voice proceeded, and, sure enough, that horrible, wandering English old maid was there.

I felt as if I could have sunk under the table for shame, seeing everyone stare at me. Anyhow, I had to bear it; and at last the lengthy meal came to an end. I went up to my room, and, for that, I saw nothing more of my acquaintances.

On the morrow I met the young girl out with her mother. When she saw me, her laughing eyes had a merrier twinkle than ever. I durst not look at her, much less follow her about as I was wont to do.

There were several other girls at the *pension,* and she soon got to be on friendly terms with them, for she was in fact a universal favorite. I, on the contrary, kept aloof from everyone, feeling sure that my mishap was not only known but had become a general topic of conversation.

One afternoon, a few days afterwards, I was in the vast garden of the *pension,* hidden behind some ilex shrubs, brooding over my ill luck, when all at once I saw Rita—for her name was Marguerite—walking in a neighboring alley, together with several other girls.

I had no sooner perceived her when she told her friends to go on, whilst she began to lag behind.

She stopped, turned her back upon her companions, lifted up her dress far above her knee, and displayed a very pretty though rather thin leg encased in a close-fitting, black silk stocking. The string which attached the stocking to her unmentionables had got undone, and she began to tie it.

By bending low I might quietly have peeped between her legs, and seen what the slit of her pantaloons afforded to the view; but it never came into my head to do so. The fact is, I had really never cared for her or for any other woman. I only thought, now is my time to find her alone and to bow to her, without having all the other girls to giggle at me. So I quietly got out of my hiding-place, and advanced towards the next alley.

As I turned the corner, what a sight did I see! There was the object of my sentimental admiration, squatted on the ground, her legs widely opened apart, her skirts all carefully tucked up.

—So at last you saw—

—A faint glimpse of pinkish flesh, and a stream of yellow liquid pouring down and flowing on the gravel, bubbling with much froth, accompanied by the rushing sound of many waters, while, as if to greet my appearance, a rumbling noise like that of an unctuous cannonade came from behind.

—And what did you do?

—Don't you know we always do the things which ought not to be done, and leave undone the things which ought to be done, as I think the Prayer Book says? So, instead of slipping away unperceived, and hiding behind a bush to try and have a glimpse at the mouth from which the rill escaped, I foolishly remained stock still, speechless, dumbfounded. It was only when she lifted up her eyes that I recovered the use of my tongue.

'Oh, mademoiselle! pardon!' said I; 'but real-

ly I did not know that you were here—that is
to say that—'

'*Sot—stupide—imbécile — bête — animal!*'
quoth she, with quite a French volubility, rising
and getting as red as a peony. Then she turned
her back on me, but only to face the wandering
old maid, who appeared at the other end of the
avenue, and who greeted her with a prolonged
'Oh!' that sounded like the blast of a fog-
trumpet.

—And—

—And the only love I ever had for a woman
thus came to an end.

3

Then you had never loved before you made
Teleny's acquaintance?

—Never; that is the reason why—for some
time—I did not quite understand what I felt.
Thinking it over, however, I afterwards came
to the conclusion that I had felt the first faint
stimulus of love already long before, but as it
had always been with my own sex, I was unconscious that this was love.

—Was it for some boy of your age?

—No, always for grown up men, for strong

muscular specimens of manhood. I had from childhood a hankering for males of the prize-fighter's type, with huge limbs, rippling muscles, mighty thews; for brutal strength, in fact.

My first infatuation was for a young Hercules of a butcher, who came courting our maid —a pretty girl, as far as I can remember. He was a stout athletic fellow with sinewy arms, who looked as if he could have felled an ox with a blow of his fist.

I often used to sit and watch him unawares, noting every expression of his face while he was making love, almost feeling the lust he felt himself.

How I did wish he would speak to me instead of joking with my stupid maid. I felt jealous of her although I liked her very much. Sometimes he used to take me up and fondle me, but that was very seldom; one day, however, when—apparently excited—he had tried hard to kiss her, and had not succeeded, he took me up and greedily pressed his lips against mine, kissing me as if he were parched with thirst.

Although I was but a very little child, still I think this act must have brought about an erection, for I remember every pulse of mine was fluttering. I still remember the pleasure I felt when—like a cat—I could rub myself against his legs, nestle between his thighs, sniff him like a dog, or pat and paddle him; but, alas! he seldom heeded me.

My greatest delight in my boyhood was to

see men bathing. I could hardly keep myself from rushing up to them; I should have liked to handle and kiss them all over. I was quite beyond myself when I saw one of them naked.

A phallus acted upon me, as—I suppose—it does upon a very hot woman; my mouth actually watered at its sight, especially if it was a good-sized, full-blooded one, with an unhooded thick and fleshy glans.

Withal, I never understood that I loved men and not women. What I felt was that convulsion of the brain that kindles the eyes with a fire full of madness, an eager bestial delight, a fierce sensual desire. Love, I thought, was a quiet drawing-room flirtation, something soft, maudlin and aesthetic, quite different from that passion full of rage and hatred which was burning within me. In a word, much more of a sedative than an aphrodisiac.

—Then, I suppose you had never had a woman?

—Oh, yes! several; though by chance, rather than by choice. Nevertheless, for a Frenchman of my age, I had begun life rather late. My mother—although considered a very light person, much given to pleasure—had taken more care of my bringing up than many serious, prosy, fussy women would have done; for she always had a great deal of tact and observation. Therefore I had never been put as a boarder into any school, for she knew that such places of education are—as a rule—only hotbeds of vice. Who is the *interne* of either sex who has not begun life by tribadism, onanism, or sodomy.

My mother, besides, was frightened lest I might have inherited my father's sensual disposition, and she, therefore, did her best to withhold from me all early temptations, and in fact she really succeeded in keeping me out of mischief.

I was therefore at fifteen and sixteen far more innocent than any of my school fellows, yet I managed to hide my utter ignorance by pretending to be more profligate and *blasé*.

Whenever they spoke of women—and they did so every day—I smiled knowingly, so that they soon came to the conclusion that 'still waters run deep.'

—And you knew absolutely nothing?

—I only knew that there was something about putting it in and pulling it out.

At fifteen, I was one day in our garden, strolling listlessly about in a little meadow by the roadside at the back of the house.

I was walking on the mossy grass, as soft as a velvety carpet, so that my footsteps were not heard. All at once I stopped by an old disused kennel, which often served me as a seat.

When I got there I heard a voice within it. I bent down my ear, and listened without moving. Thereupon I heard a young girl's voice say:

'Put it in and then pull it out; then put it in again, and pull it out; and so on for some time.'

'But I can't put it in,' was the reply.

'Now,' said the first. 'I open my hole widely

with both my hands. Push it in; stick it in—
more—much more—as much as you can.'

'Well—but take away your fingers.'

'There—it's all out again; try and push it in.'

'But I can't. Your hole is shut,' muttered the boy's voice.

'Press down.'

'But why have I to put it in?'

'Well, you see my sister has a soldier for her good friend; and they always do like that when they are alone together. Haven't you seen the cocks jump on the hens, and peck at them? Well, they also do like that, only my sister and the soldier kiss and kiss; so that it takes them a long time to do it.'

'And he always puts it in and pulls it out?'

'Of course; only just at the end my sister always tells him to mind and not finish it in her, so that he may not make her a child. So now, if you wish to be my good friend—as you say you want—push it in—with your fingers, if you can't otherwise; but pay attention and don't finish in me, because you may make me a child.'

Thereupon I peeped in, and I saw our gardener's youngest daughter—a girl of ten or twelve—stretched on her back, while a little vagrant of about seven was sprawling over her, trying his best to put her instructions into practice.

That was my first lesson, and I had thereby a faint inkling of what men and women do when they are lovers.

—And you were not curious to know more about the matter?

—Oh, yes! Many a time I should have yielded to the temptation, and have accompanied my friends in their visit to some wenches—whose charms they always extolled in a peculiar low, nasal, goatish voice, and with an unexplainable shivering of the whole body—had I not been kept back by the fear of being laughed at by them and by the girls themselves; for I should still have been as inexperienced in knowing what to do with a woman as Daphnis himself, before Lycenion had slipped under him, and thus initiated him into the mysteries of love; and yet hardly more initiation is required in the matter than for the new-born babe to take to the breast.

—But when did your first visit to a brothel take place?

—Upon leaving college, when the mystic laurel and bays had wreathed our brows. According to tradition we were to partake of a farewell supper and make jolly together, before separating on our divers paths in life.

—Yes, I remember those merry suppers of the Quartier Latin.

—When the supper was over—

—And everyone more or less tipsy—

—Precisely; it was agreed that we should pass the evening in visiting some of the houses of nightly entertainment. Although I was myself rather merry, and usually up to any kind of joke, still I felt somewhat shy, and would willingly have given my friends the slip, rather than expose myself to their ridicule and to all the horrors of syphilis; but do what I could it was impossible to get rid of them.

They called me a sneak, they imagined that I wanted to spend the evening with some mistress, a pretty *grisette*, or a fashionable *cocotte*, for the term *horizontale* had not yet come into fashion. Another hinted that I was tied to my mammy's apron-strings, that my dad had not allowed me to take the latch-key. A third said that I wanted to go and *'menarmi la rilla'* as Aretino crudely expresses it.

Seeing that it was impossible to escape, I consented with a good grace to accompany them.

A certain Biou, young in years, but old in craft, who—like an elderly tomcat—had, at sixteen, already lost an eye in a battle of love, (having got some syphilitic virus into it), proposed to show us life in the unknown parts of the real Quartier Latin.

'First,' said he, 'I'll take you to a place where we'll spend little and have some jolly fun; it'll just put us *"en train"* and from there we'll go to another house, to fire off our pistols, or I should rather say our revolvers, for mine is a seven shot barrel.'

His single eye twinkled with delight, and his trousers were stirred from within as he said this. We all agreed to his proposal, I especially feeling quite glad that I might at first remain only a spectator. I wondered, however, what the sight would be like.

We had an endless drive through the narrow straggling streets, alleys, and by-ways, where painted women appeared in gorgeous dresses at the filthy windows of some wretched houses.

As it was getting late, all the shops were now shut, except the fruiterers, who sold fried fish, mussels, and potatoes. These disgorged an offensive smell of dirt, grease, and hot oil, which mixed itself up with the stench of the gutters and that of the cesspools in the middle of the streets.

In the darkness of the ill-lighted thoroughfares more than one *café chantant* and beerhouse flared with red gaslights, and as we passed them we felt the puffs of warm, close air reeking with alcohol, tobacco, and sour beer.

All those streets were thronged with a motley crowd. There were tipsy men with scowling, ugly faces, slipshod vixens, and pale, precociously withered children all tattered and torn, singing obscene songs.

At last we came to a kind of slum, where the carriages stopped before a low, beetling-browed house which seemed to have suffered from water on the brain when a child. It had a crazy look; and being, moreover, painted in yellowish-red, its many excoriations gave it the appearance of having some loathsome, scabby, skin disease. This place of infamous resort seemed to forewarn the visitor of the illness festering within its walls.

We went in at a small door, up a winding, greasy, slippery staircase, lighted by an asthmatic, flickering gaslight. Although I was loath to lay my hand on the bannisters, it was almost impossible to mount those muddy stairs without doing so.

On the first landing we were greeted by a grey-haired old hag, with a bloated yet bloodless face. I really do not know what made her so repulsive to me—perhaps it was her sore and lashless eyes, her mean expression, or her trade—but the fact is, I had never in all my life seen such a ghoul-like creature. Her mouth with its toothless gums and its hanging lips seemed like the sucker of some polypus; it was so foul and slimy.

She welcomed us with many low curtsies and fawning words of endearment, and ushered us into a low and tawdry room, where a flaring petroleum light shed its crude sheen all around.

Some frowsy curtains at the windows, a few old armchairs, and a long, battered, and muchstained divan completed the furniture of this room, which had a mixed stench of musk and onions; but, as I was just then gifted with a rather strong imagination, I at times detected— or I thought I did—a smell of carbolic acid and of iodine; albeit the loathsome smell of musk overpowered all other odors.

In this den, several—what shall I call them? —sirens? no harpies! were crouched, or lolled about.

Although I tried to put on a most indifferent,

blasé look, still my face must have expressed all the horror I felt. This is then, said I to myself, one of those delightful houses of pleasure, of which I have heard so many glowing tales?

These painted-up Jezebels, cadaverous or bloated, are the Paphian maids, the splendid votaresses of Venus, whose magic charms make the senses thrill with delight, the houris on whose breasts you swoon away and are ravished into paradise.

My friends seeing my utter bewilderment began to laugh at me. I thereupon sat down and tried stupidly to smile.

Three of those creatures at once came up to me; one of them, putting her arms round my neck, kissed me, and wanted to dart her filthy tongue into my mouth; the others began to handle me most indecently. The more I resisted, the more bent they seemed on making a Laocoon of me.

—But why were you singled out as their victim?

—I really do not know, but it must have been because I looked so innocently scared, or because my friends were all laughing at my horror-stricken face.

One of those poor women—a tall dark girl, an Italian, I believe—was evidently in the very last stage of consumption. She was in fact a mere skeleton, and still—had it not been for the mask of chalk and red with which her face was covered—traces of a former beauty might still have been discerned in her; seeing her now, anyone not inured to such sights could not but feel a sense of the deepest pity.

The second was red-haired, gaunt, pock-marked, goggle-eyed and repulsive.

The third: old, short, squat and obese; quite a bladder of fat. She went by the name of the *cantinière*.

The first was dressed in grass-green, or prassino; the red-haired strumpet wore a robe which once must have been blue; the old slut was clad in yellow.

All these dresses, however, were stained and very much the worse for wear. Besides, some slimy viscid fluid which had left large spots everywhere, made them seem as if all the snails of Burgundy had been crawling over them.

I managed to get rid of the two younger ones, but I was not so successful with the *cantinière*.

Having seen that her charms, and all her little endearments, had no effect upon me, she tried to rouse my sluggish senses by more desperate means.

As I said before, I was sitting upon the low divan; she thereupon stood in front of me and pulled her dress up to her waist, thus exhibiting all her hitherto hidden attractions. It was the first time I had seen a naked woman, and this one was positively loathsome. And yet, now that I think of it, her beauty might well be compared with that of the Shulamite, for her neck was like the tower of David, her navel resembled a round goblet, her belly a huge heap of blighted wheat. Her hair, beginning from her waist and falling down to her knees, was not exactly like a flock of goats—as the hair of Solomon's bride—but in quantity it surely was like that of a good-sized black sheepskin.

Her legs—similar to those described in the biblical song—were two massive columns straight up and down, without any sign of calf or ankle about them. Her whole body, in fact, was one bulky mass of quivering fat. If her smell was not quite that of Lebanon it was surely of musk, patchouli, stale fish and perspiration; but as my nose came in closer contact with the fleece, the smell of stale fish predominated.

She stood for a minute in front of me; then, coming nearer by a step or two, put one foot on the divan, and opening her legs as she did so, she took my head between her fat, clammy hands.

'Viens mon chéri, fais minette à ton petit chat.'

As she said this I saw the black mass of hair part itself; two huge dark lips first appeared, then opened, and within those bulgy lips — which inside had the color and the look of stale butcher's meat—I saw something like the tip of a dog's penis when in a state of erection, protrude itself towards my lips.

All my schoolfellows burst out laughing— why, I did not exactly understand; for I had not the slightest idea of what *minette* was, or what the old whore wanted of me; nor could I see that anything so loathsome could be turned into a joke.

—Well, and how did that jolly evening come to an end?

—Drinks had been ordered—beer, spirits, and some bottles of frothy stuff, yclept champagne, which surely was not the produce of the sunny wines of France, but of which the women imbibed copiously.

After this, not wishing us to leave the house without having been entertained in some way or other, and to get a few more francs out of our pockets, they proposed to show us some tricks that they could do amongst themselves.

It was apparently a rare sight, and the one for which we had come to this house. My friends acquiesced unanimously. Thereupon the old bladder of fat undressed herself stark naked, and shook her buttocks in a kind of poor imitation of the Eastern Dance of the Wasp. The poor consumptive wretch followed her example, and slipped off her dress by a simple shake of her body.

At the sight of that huge mass of flabby hog's lard flapping on either side of the rump, the thin whore lifted up her hand, and gave her friend a smart slap on the buttocks, but the hand seemed to sink in, as into a mass of butter.

'Ah!' said the *cantinière*; 'this is the little game you like, is it?'

And she answered the blow by a smarter one on her friend's backside.

Thereupon the consumptive girl began to run

round the room, and the *cantinière* toddled after her in the most provoking attitude, each trying to slap the other.

As the old prostitute passed Biou, he gave her a loud smack with his open palm, and soon after, most of the other students followed suit, evidently much excited by this little game of flagellation, until the buttocks of the two women were of a crimson red.

The *cantinière* having at last managed to seize her friend, she sat down, and laid her across her knees, saying, 'Now, my friend, you will get it to your heart's content.'

And suiting the action to the words, she belabored her soundly; that is, striking her as strongly as her chubby little hands allowed her.

The young woman having at last succeeded in getting up, both the women thereupon began to kiss and fondle each other. Then, with thighs against thighs and breasts against breasts, they stood a moment in that position; after which, they brushed aside the bushy hair that covered the lower part of the so-called Mount of Venus, and opening their thick brown and bulgy lips, they placed one clitoris in contact with the other, and these as they touched wagged with delight; then, encircling their arms round each other's backs, with their mouths close together, breathing each other's fetid breath, the one sucking alternately the other's tongue, they began to rub mightily together. They twisted, they writhed, and they shook, putting themselves into all kinds of contortions for some time, yet hardly able to stand on account of the intensity of the rapture they felt.

At last, the consumptive girl, clasping with her hands the backside of the other one, and thus opening the huge pulpy buttocks, called out:

'Une feuille de rose.'

Of course I greatly wondered what she meant, and I asked myself where she could find a rose-leaf, for there was not a flower to be seen in the house; and then I said to myself—having got one what will she do with it?

I was not left to wonder long, for the *cant-inière* did to her friend what she had done to her. Thereupon two other whores came and knelt down before the backsides that were thus held open for them, and began to lick them, to the pleasure of the active and passive prostitutes, and to that of all the lookers-on.

Moreover, the kneeling women, thrusting their forefingers between the legs of the standing strumpets and on the lower extremity of the lips, began to rub vigorously.

The consumptive girl thus masturbated, kissed, rubbed, and licked, began to writhe furiously, to pant, to sob and to scream with joy, delight, and almost pain, until half fainting.

'Aïe, là, là, assez, aïe, c'est fait,' followed by cries, screams, monosyllables, and utterances of keen delight and unbearable pleasure.

'Now it is my turn,' said the *cantinière*, and stretching herself on the low couch, she opened her legs wide so that the two thick dark lips gaped, and disclosed a clitoris which in its erection was of such a size, that in my ignorance I concluded this woman to be an hermaphrodite.

Her friend, the other *gougnotte*—this was the first time I had heard the expression—though hardly recovered, went and placed her head between the *cantinière's* legs, lips against lips, and her tongue on the stiff, red, moist, and wagging clitoris, she too being in such a position that her own middle parts were in the reach of the other whore's mouth.

They wriggled and moved, they rubbed and bumped each other, and their dishevelled hair spread itself not only on the couch but also on the floor; they clasped each other, squeezed the nipples of their breasts, and dug their nails into the fleshy parts of their bodies, for in their erotic fury they were like two wild Maenads, and only smothered their cries in the fury of their kisses.

Though their lust seemed to grow even stronger, still it did not overcome them, and the fat and tough old strumpet in her eagerness to enjoy was now pressing down her lover's head with both her hands and with all her might, as if she were actually trying to get it all in her womb.

The sight was really loathsome, and I turned my head aside so as not to see it, but the view that offered itself all around was, if anything, more disgusting.

The whores had unbuttoned all the young men's trousers, some were handling their organs, caressing their testicles or licking their backsides; one was kneeling before a young student and greedily sucking his huge and fleshy phallus, another girl was sitting astraddle a young man's knees, springing up and coming down again as if she had been in a baby-jumper —evidently running a Paphian race, and (perhaps there were not enough prostitutes, or it was done for the fun of the thing) one woman was being had by two men at the same time, one in front, the other behind. There were also other enormities, but I had not time enough to see everything.

Moreover, many of the young men who were already tipsy when they came here, having drunk champagne, absinthe and beer, began now to feel squeamish, to be quite sick, to hiccough, and finally to throw up.

In the midst of this nauseous scene, the consumptive whore went off into a fit of hysterics, crying and sobbing at the same time, while the fat one who was now thoroughly excited would not allow her to lift her head; and having got her nose where the tongue had hitherto been, she was rubbing herself against it with all her might, screaming:

'Lick on, lick stronger, don't take away your tongue now that I am about to enjoy it; there, I am finishing, lick on, suck me, bite me.'

But the poor cadaverous wretch in the paroxysm of her delirium had managed to slip away her head.

'Regarde donc quel con,' said Biou, pointing

to that mass of quivering flesh amidst the black and froth-covered viscid hair. 'I shall just get my knee into it, and rub her soundly. Now, you'll see!'

He pulled off his trousers, and was about to suit the action to the words, when a slight cough was heard. It was at once followed by a piercing cry; and before we could understand what was the matter, the body of the tough old prostitute was bathed in blood. The cadaverous wretch had in a fit of lubricity broken a blood vessel, and was dying—dying—dead!

'*Ah! la sale bougre!*' said the ghoul-like woman with the bloodless face. 'It's all over with the slut now, and she owes me . . .'

I do not remember the sum she mentioned. In the meanwhile, however, the *cantinière* continued to writhe in her senseless and ungovernable rage, twisting and distorting herself; but at last, feeling the warm blood flow in her womb, and bathe her inflamed parts, she began to pant, to scream, and to leap with delight, for the ejaculation was at length taking place.

Thus it happened that the death-rattle of the one mixed itself up with the panting and gurgling of the other.

In that confusion I slipped away, cured forever of the temptation of again visiting such a house of nightly entertainment.

L et us now go back to our story.

—When was it that you met Teleny again?

—Not for some time afterwards. The fact is that although I continued to feel irresistibly attracted towards him, drawn as it were by an impelling power the strength of which I could at times hardly withstand, still I continued to avoid him.

Whenever he played in public I always went to hear him—or rather, to look at him; and I only lived during those short moments when he was on the stage. My glasses would then be rivetted upon him; my eyes gloated upon his heavenly figure, so full of youth, life, and manhood.

The longing that I felt to press my mouth on his beautiful mouth and parted lips was so intense that it always made my penis water.

At times the space between us seemed to lessen and dwindle in such a way that I felt as though I could breathe his warm and scented breath—nay, I actually seemed to feel the contact of his body against my own.

The sensation produced by the mere thought that his skin was touching mine excited my nervous system in such a way that the intensity of this barren pleasure produced at first a pleasant numbness over my whole body, which, being prolonged, soon turned into a dull pain.

He himself always appeared to feel my presence in the theatre, for his eyes invariably looked for me until they pierced the densest crowd to find me out. I knew, however, that he could not really see me in the corner where I was ensconced, either in the pit, the gallery, or at the bottom of some box. Still, go, whithersoever I would, his glances were always directed towards me. Ah, those eyes! as unfathomable as the dim water of a well. Even now, as I remember them after these many years, my heart beats, and I feel my head grow giddy thinking of them. If you had seen those eyes, you would know what that burning languor which poets are always writing about really is.

Of one thing I was justly proud. Since that

famous evening of the charity concert, he played—if not in a more theoretically correct way—far more brilliantly and more sensationally than he had ever done before.

His whole heart now poured itself out in those voluptuous Hungarian melodies, and all those whose blood was not frozen with envy and age were entranced by that music.

His name, therefore, began to attract large audiences, and although musical critics were divided in their opinions, the papers always had long articles about him.

—And—being so much in love with him—you had the fortitude to suffer, and yet to resist the temptation of seeing him.

—I was young and inexperienced, therefore moral; for what is morality but prejudice?

—Prejudice?

—Well, is nature moral? Does the dog that smells and licks with evident gusto the first bitch that he meets, trouble his unsophisticated brain with morality? Does the poodle that endeavors to sodomize that little cur coming across the street care what a canine Mrs. Grundy will say about him?

No, unlike poodles, or young Arabs, I had been inculcated with all kinds of wrong ideas, so when I understood what my natural feelings for Teleny were, I was staggered, horrified; and filled with dismay, I resolved to stifle them.

Indeed, had I known human nature better, I should have left France, gone to the antipodes, placed the Himalayas as a barrier between us.

—Only to yield to your natural tastes with someone else, or with him, had you happened to meet unexpectedly after many years.

—You are quite right; physiologists tell us that the body of man changes after seven years; a man's passions, however, remain always the same; though smouldering in a latent state, they are in his bosom all the same; his nature is surely no better because he has not given vent to them. He is only humbugging himself and cheating everybody by pretending to be what he is not; I know that I was born a sodomite, the fault is my constitution's, not mine own.

I read all I could find about the love of one man for another, that loathsome crime against nature taught to us not only by the very gods themselves, but by all the greatest men of olden times, for even Minos himself seems to have sodomized Theseus.

I, of course, looked upon it as a monstrosity, a sin—as Origen says—far worse than idolatry. And yet I had to admit that the world—even after the cities of the plain had been destroyed —throve well enough notwithstanding this aberration, for Paphian girls in the great days of Rome were but too often discarded for pretty little boys.

It was but time for Christianity to come and sweep away all the monstrous vices of this world with its brand new broom. Catholicism later on burnt those men who sowed in a sterile field—in effigy.

The popes had their catamites, the kings had their *mignons,* and if all the host of priests, monks, friars and caluyers were forgiven, they —it must be admitted—did not always commit buggery, or cast away their seed on rocky soil, although religion did not intend their implements to be baby-making tools.

As for the Templars, if they were burnt, it surely could not have been on account of their pederasty, for it had been winked at long enough.

What amused me, however, was to see that every writer impeached all his neighbors of indulging in this abomination; his own people alone were free from this shocking vice.

The Jews accused the Gentiles, and the Gentiles the Jews, and—like syphilis—all the black sheep who had this perverted taste had always imported it from abroad. I also read in a modern medical book, how the penis of a sodomite becomes thin and pointed like a dog's, and how the human mouth gets distorted when used for vile purposes, and I shuddered with horror and disgust. Even the sight of that book blanched my cheek!

It is true that since then, experience has taught me quite another lesson, for I must confess that I have known scores of whores, and many other women besides, who have used their mouths not only for praying and for kissing their confessor's hand, and yet I have never perceived that their mouths were crooked, have you?

As for my penis, or yours, its bulky head—but you blush at the compliment, so we will drop this subject.

At that time I tortured my brain, fearing to have committed this heinous sin morally, if not materially.

Mosaic religion, rendered stricter by the Talmudic law, has invented a cowl to be used in the act of copulation. It wraps up the whole body of the husband, leaving in the middle of the gown but a tiny hole—like that in a little boy's pants—to pass the penis through, and thus enable him to squirt his sperm into his wife's ovaries, fecundating her in this way, but preventing as much as possible all carnal pleasure. Ah, yes! but people have long since taken French leave of the cowl, hoodwinking the whole affair by hooding their falcon with a 'French letter.'

Yes, but are we not born with a leaden cowl —namely, this Mosaic religion of ours, improved upon by Christ's mystic precepts, and rendered impossible, perfect, by Protestant hypocrisy; for if a man commits adultery with a woman every time he looks at her, did I not commit sodomy with Teleny every time I saw him or even thought of him?

There were moments however when, nature being stronger than prejudice, I should right willingly have given up my soul to perdition—nay, yielded my body to suffer in eternal hell-fire—if in the meanwhile I could have fled somewhere on the confines of this earth, on some lonely island, where in perfect nakedness I could have lived for some years in deadly sin with him, feasting upon his fascinating beauty.

Still I resolved to keep aloof from him, to be his motive power, his guiding spirit, to make of him a great, a famous, artist. As for the fire of lewdness burning within me—well, if I could not extinguish it, I could at least subdue it.

I suffered. My thoughts, night and day, were with him. My brain was always aglow; my blood was overheated; my body ever shivering with excitement. I daily read all the newspapers to see what they said about him; and whenever his name met my eyes the paper shook in my trembling hands. If my mother or anybody else mentioned his name I blushed and then grew pale.

I remember what a shock of pleasure, not unmingled with jealousy, I felt, when for the first time I saw his likeness in a window amongst those of other celebrities. I went and bought it at once, not simply to treasure and dote upon it, but also that other people might not look at it.

—What! you were so very jealous?

—Foolishly so. Unseen and at a distance I used to follow him about, after every concert he played.

Usually he was alone. Once, however, I saw him enter a cab waiting at the back door of the theatre. It had seemed to me as if someone else was within the vehicle—a woman, if I had not been mistaken. I hailed another cab, and followed them. Their carriage stopped at Teleny's house. I at once bade my Jehu do the same.

I saw Teleny alight. As he did so, he offered his hand to a lady, thickly veiled, who tripped out of the carriage and darted into the open doorway. The cab then went off.

I bade my driver wait there the whole night. At dawn the carriage of the evening before came and stopped. My driver looked up. A few minutes afterwards the door was again opened. The lady hurried out, was handed into her carriage by her lover. I followed her, and stopped where she alighted.

A few days afterwards I knew whom she was.

—And who was she?

—A lady of an unblemished reputation with whom Teleny had played some duets.

In the cab, that night, my mind was so intently fixed upon Teleny that my inward self seemed to disintegrate itself from my body and to follow like his own shadow the man I loved. I unconsciously threw myself into a kind of trance and I had a most vivid hallucination, which, strange as it might appear, coincided with all that my friend did and felt.

For instance, as soon as the door was shut behind them, the lady caught Teleny in her arms, and gave him a long kiss. Their entrance would have lasted several seconds more had Teleny not lost his breath.

You smile; yes, I suppose you yourself are aware how easily people lose their breath in kissing, when the lips do not feel that blissful intoxicating lust in all its intensity. She would have given him another kiss, but Teleny whispered to her: 'Let us go up to my room; there we shall be far safer than here.'

Soon they were in his apartment.

She looked timidly around, and seeing herself in that young man's room alone with him, she blushed and seemed thoroughly ashamed of herself.

'Oh! René,' she said, 'what must you think of me?'

'That you love me dearly,' quoth he; 'do you not?'

'Yes, indeed; not wisely, but too well.'

Thereupon taking off her wrappers, she rushed up and clasped her lover in her arms, showering her warm kisses on his head, his eyes, his cheeks and then upon his mouth. That mouth I so longed to kiss!

With lips pressed together, she remained for some time inhaling his breath, and—almost frightened at her boldness—she touched his lips with the tip of her tongue. Then, taking courage, soon afterwards she slipped it in his mouth, and then after a while, she thrust it in and out, as if she were enticing him to try the act of nature by it; she was so convulsed with lust by this kiss that she had to clasp herself to him not to fall, for the blood was rushing to her head, and her knees were almost giving way beneath her. At last, taking his right hand, after squeezing it hesitatingly for a moment, she placed it upon her breasts, giving him her nipple to pinch, and as he did so, the pleasure she felt was so great that she was swooning away for joy.

'Oh, Teleny!' she said; 'I can't! I can't any more.'

And she rubbed herself as strongly as she could against him, protruding her middle parts against his.

—And Teleny?

—Well, jealous as I was, I could not help feeling how different his manner was now from the rapturous way with which he had clung to me that evening, when he had taken the bunch of heliotrope from his buttonhole and had put it in mine.

He accepted rather than returned her caresses. Anyhow, she seemed pleased, for she thought him shy.

She was now hanging on him. One of her arms was clasped around his waist, the other one around his neck. Her dainty, tapering, bejewelled fingers were playing with his curly hair, and paddling his neck.

He was squeezing her breasts, and, as I said before, slightly fingering her nipples.

She gazed deep into his eyes, and then sighed.

'You do not love me,' she said at last. 'I can see it in your eyes. You are not thinking of me, but of somebody else.'

And it was true. At that moment he was thinking of me—fondly, longingly; and then, as he did so, he got more excited, and he caught her in his arms, and hugged and kissed her with

far more eagerness than he had hitherto done—
nay, he began to suck her tongue as if it had
been mine, and then began to thrust his own
into her mouth.

After a few moments of rapture she, this
time, stopped to take a breath.

'Yes, I am wrong. You love me. I see it now.
You do not despise me because I am here, do
you?'

'Ah! if you could only read in my heart, and
see how madly I love you, darling!'

And she looked at him with longing, passionate eyes.

'Still you think me light, don't you? I am an
adulteress!'

And thereupon she shuddered, and hid her
face in her hands.

He looked at her for a moment pitifully, then
he took down her hands gently, and kissed her.

'You do not know how I have tried to resist
you, but I could not. I am on fire. My blood is
no longer blood, but some burning love-philter.
I cannot help myself,' said she, lifting up her
head defiantly as if she were facing the whole
world, 'here I am, do with me what you like, only
tell me that you love me, that you love no other
woman but me, swear it.'

'I swear,' he said languidly, 'that I love no
other woman.'

She did not understand the meaning of his
words.

'But tell it to me again, say it often, it is so
sweet to hear it repeated from the lips of those

we dote on,' said she, with passionate eagerness.

'I assure you that I have never cared for any woman so much as I do for you.'

'Cared?' said she, disappointed.

'Loved, I mean.'

'And you can swear it?'

'On the cross if you like,' he added, smiling.

'And you do not think badly of me because I am here? Well, you are the only one for whom I have ever been unfaithful to my husband; though God knows if he be faithful—my husband; God knows if he be faithful to me. Still my love does not atone for my sin, does it?'

Teleny did not give her any answer for an instant, he looked at her with dreamy eyes, then shuddered as if awaking from a trance.

'Sin,' he said, 'is the only thing worth living for.'

She looked at him rather astonished, but then she kissed him again and again and answered: 'Well, yes, you are perhaps right; it is so, the fruit of the forbidden tree was pleasant to the sight, to the taste, and to the smell.'

They sat down on a divan. When they were clasped again in each other's arms he slipped his hand somewhat timidly and almost unwillingly under her skirts.

She caught hold of his hand, and arrested it.

'No, René, I beg of you! Could we not love each other with a Platonic love? Is that not enough?'

'Is it enough for you?' said he, almost superciliously.

She pressed her lips again upon his, and almost relinquished her grasp. The hand went stealthily up along the leg, stopped a moment on the knees, caressing them; but the legs closely pressed together prevented it from slipping between them, and thus reaching the higher story. It crept up, nevertheless, caressing the thighs through the fine linen underclothing, and thus, by stolen marches, it reached its aim. The hand then slipped between the opening of the drawers, and began to feel the soft skin. She tried to stop him.

'No, no!' she said; 'please don't; you are tickling me.'

He then took courage, and plunged his fingers boldly in the fine curly locks of the fleece that covered all her middle parts.

She continued to hold her thighs tightly closed together, especially when the naughty fingers began to graze the edge of the moist lips. At that touch, however, her strength gave way; the nerves relaxed and allowed the tip of a finger to worm its way within the slit—nay, the tiny berry protruded out to welcome it.

After a few moments she breathed more strongly. She encircled his breast with her arms, kissed him, and then hid her head on his shoulder.

'Oh, what a rapture I feel!' she cried. 'What a magnetic fluid you possess to make me feel I as do!'

He did not give her any answer; but, unbuttoning his trousers, he took hold of her dainty little hand. He endeavored to introduce it within the gap. She tried to resist, but weakly, and as if asking but to yield. She soon gave way, and boldly caught hold of his phallus, now stiff and hard, moving lustily by its own inward strength.

After a few moments of pleasant manipulation, their lips pressed together, he lightly, and almost against her knowledge, pressed her down on the couch, lifted up her legs, pulled up her skirts without for a moment taking his tongue out of her mouth or stopping his tickling of her tingling clitoris already wet with its own tears. Then—sustaining his weight on his elbows—he got his legs between her thighs. That her excitement increased could be easily seen by the shivering of the lips which he had no need to open as he pressed down upon her, for they parted of themselves to give entrance to the little blind God of Love.

With one thrust he introduced himself within the precincts of Love's temple; with another, the rod was halfway in; with the third he reached the very bottom of the den of pleasure; for, though she was no longer in the first days of earliest youth, still she had hardly reached her prime, and her flesh was not only firm, but she was so tight that he was fairly clasped and sucked by those pulpy lips; so, after moving up and down a few times, thrusting himself always further, he crushed her down with his full weight; for both his hands were either handling her breasts, or else, having slipped them under her, squeezing her buttocks; thus wedging her on both sides, making her feel a more intense pleasure.

After a few seconds of this little game he began to breathe strongly—to pant. The milky fluid that had for days accumulated itself now rushed out in thick jets, coursing up into her very womb. She, thus flooded, showed her hysteric enjoyment by her screams, her tears, her sighs. Finally, all strength gave way; arms and legs stiffened themselves; she fell lifeless on the couch; while he remained stretched over her at the risk of giving the Count, her husband, an heir of gipsy blood.

He soon recovered his strength and rose. She was then recalled to her senses, but only to melt into a flood of tears.

A bumper of champagne brought them both, however, to a less gloomy sense of life. A few partridge sandwiches, some lobster patties, a caviar salad, with a few more glasses of champagne, together with many *marrons glacés*, and a punch made of maraschino, pineapple juice and whisky, drunk out of the same goblet soon finished by dispelling their gloominess.

'Why should we not put ourselves at our ease, my dear?' said he. 'I'll set you the example, shall I?'

'By all means.'

Thereupon Teleny took off his white tie, that stiff and uncomfortable, useless appendage invented by fashion only to torture mankind, yclept a shirt collar, then his coat and waistcoat, and he remained only in his shirt and trousers.

'Now, my dear, allow me to act as your maid.'

The beautiful woman at first refused, but yielded after some kisses; and little by little, nothing was left of all her clothing but an almost transparent *crêpe de Chine* chemise, dark steel-blue silk stockings, and satin slippers.

Teleny covered her bare neck and arms with kisses, pressed his cheeks against the thick, black hair of her armpits, and tickled her as he did so. This little titillation was felt all over her body, and the slit between her legs opened again in such a way that the delicate little clitoris, like a red hawthorn berry, peeped out as if to see what was going on. He held her for a moment crushed against his chest, and his *'merle'*—as the Italians call it—flying out of his cage, he thrust it into the opening ready to receive it.

She pushed lustily against him, but he had to keep her up, for her legs were almost giving away, so great was the pleasure she felt. He therefore stretched her down on the panther rug at his feet, without unclasping her.

All sense of shyness was now overcome. He pulled off his clothes, and pressed down with all his strength. She—to receive his instrument far in her sheath—clasped him with her legs in such a way that he could hardly move. He was, therefore, only able to rub himself against her; but that was more than enough, for after a few violent shakes of their buttocks, legs pressed, and breasts crushed, the burning liquid which he injected within her body gave her a spasmodic pleasure, and she fell senseless on the panther skin while he rolled, motionless, by her side.

Till then I felt that my image had always been present before his eyes, although he was enjoying this handsome woman—so beautiful, for she had hardly yet reached the bloom of ripe womanhood; but now the pleasure she had given him had made him quite forget me. I therefore hated him. For a moment I felt that I should like to be a wild beast—to drive my nails into his flesh, to torture him like a cat does a mouse, and to tear him into pieces.

What right had he to love anybody but myself? Did I love a single being in this world as I loved him? Could I feel pleasure with anyone else?

No, my love was not a maudlin sentimentality, it was the maddening passion that overpowers the body and shatters the brain!

If he could love women, why did he then make love to me, obliging me to love him, making me a contemptible being in my own eyes?

In the paroxysm of my excitement I writhed, I bit my lips till they bled. I dug my nails into my flesh; I cried out with jealousy and shame. I wanted but little to have made me jump out of the cab, and go and ring at the door of his house.

This state of things lasted for a few moments, and then I began to wonder what he was doing, and the fit of hallucination came over me again.

I saw him awakening from the slumber into which he had fallen when overpowered by enjoyment.

As he awoke he looked at her. Now I could see her plainly, for I believe that she was only visible to me through his medium.

—But you fell asleep, and dreamt all this whilst you were in the cab, did you not?

—Oh, no! All happened as I am telling you. I related my whole vision to him some time afterwards, and he acknowledged that everything had occurred exactly as I had seen it.

—But how could this be?

—There was, as I told you before, a strong transmission of thoughts between us. This is by no means a remarkable coincidence. You smile and look incredulous; well follow the doings of the Psychical Society, and this vision will certainly not astonish you any more.

—Well, never mind, go on.

—As Teleny awoke, he looked at his mistress lying on the panther-skin at his side.

She was as sound asleep as anyone would be after a banquet, intoxicated by strong drink; or as a baby, that having sucked its fill, stretches itself glutted by the side of its mother's breast. It was the heavy sleep of lusty life, not the placid stillness of cold death. The blood—like the sap of a young tree in spring—mounted to her parted, pouting lips, through which a warm scented breath escaped at cadenced intervals, emitting that slight murmur which the child hears as he listens in a shell—the sound of slumbering life.

The breasts—as if swollen with milk—stood up, and the erect nipples seemed to be asking for those caresses she was so fond of; over all her body there was a shivering of insatiable desire.

Her thighs were bare, and the thick curly hair that covered her middle parts, as black as jet, was sprinkled over with pearly drops of milky dew.

Such a sight would have awakened an eager, irrepressible desire in Joseph himself, the only chaste Israelite of whom we have ever heard; and yet Teleny, leaning on his elbow, was gazing at her with all the loathsomeness we feel when we look at a kitchen table covered with the offal of the meat, the hashed scraps, the dregs of the wines which have supplied the banquet that has just glutted us.

He looked at her with the scorn which a man has for the woman who has just ministered to his pleasure, and who has degraded herself and him. Moreover, as he felt unjust towards her, he hated her, and not himself.

I felt again that he did not love her, but me, though she had made him for a few moments forget me.

She seemed to feel his cold glances upon her, for she shivered, and, thinking she was asleep in bed, she tried to cover herself up; and her hand, fumbling for the sheet, pulled up her chemise, only uncovering herself more by that action. She awoke as she did so, and caught Teleny's reproachful glances.

She looked around, frightened. She tried to cover herself as much as she could; and then, entwining one of her arms round the young man's neck—

'Do not look at me like that,' she said. 'Am I so loathsome to you? Oh! I see it. You despise me.' And her eyes filled with tears. 'You are right. Why did I yield? Why did I not resist the love that was torturing me? Alas! it was not you; but I who sought you, who made love to you; and now you feel for me nothing but disgust. Tell me, is it so? You love another woman! No!—tell me you don't!'

'I don't,' said Teleny earnestly.

'Yes, but swear.'

'I have already sworn before, or at least offered to do so. What is the use of swearing, if you don't believe me?'

Though all lust was gone, Teleny felt a heartfelt pity for that handsome young woman who, maddened by love for him, had put into jeopardy her whole existence to throw herself into his arms.

Who is the man that is not flattered by the love he inspires in a high-born, wealthy, and handsome young woman, who forgets her marriage to enjoy a few moments of bliss in his arms? But then, why do women generally love men who often care so little for them?

Teleny did his best to comfort her, to tell her over and over again that he cared for no woman, to assure her that he would be eternally faithful to her for her sacrifice; but pity is not love, nor is affection the eagerness of desire.

Nature was more than satisfied; her beauty had lost all its attraction; they kissed again and again; he languidly passed his hands over all her body, from the nape of the neck to the deep dent between those round hills, which seemed covered with fallen snow, giving her a most delightful sensation as he did so; he caressed her breasts, suckled and bit the tiny protruding nipples, while his fingers were often thrust far within the warm flesh hidden under that mass of jet-black hair. She glowed, she breathed, she shivered with pleasure; but Teleny, though performing his work with masterly skill, remained cold at her side.

'No, I see that you don't love me; for it is not possible that you—a young man—'

She did not finish. Teleny felt the sting of her reproaches, but remained passive; for the phallus is not stiffened by taunts.

She took the lifeless object in her delicate fingers. She rubbed and manipulated it. She even rolled it between her two soft hands. It remained like a piece of dough. She sighed as piteously as Ovid's mistress must have done on a like occasion. She did like this woman did some hundreds of years before. She bent down; she took the tip of that inert piece of flesh between her lips—the pulpy lips which looked like a tiny apricot—so round, sappy, and luscious. Soon it was all in her mouth. She sucked it with as much evident pleasure as if she were a famished baby taking her nurse's breast. As it went in and out, she tickled the prepuce with her expert tongue, touched the tiny lips on her palate.

The phallus, though somewhat harder, remained always limp and nerveless.

You know our ignorant forefathers believed in the practice called *'nouer les aiguillettes'*—that is rendering the male incapable of performing the pleasant work for which Nature has destined him. We, the enlightened generation, have discarded such gross superstitions, and still our ignorant forefathers were sometimes right.

—What! you do not mean to say that you believe in such tomfoolery?

—It might be tomfoolery, as you say; but still it is a fact. Hypnotize a person, and then you will see if you can get the mastery over him or not.

—Still, you had not hypnotized Teleny?

—No, but our natures seemed to be bound to one another by a secret affinity.

At that moment I felt a secret shame for Teleny. Not being able to understand the working of his brain, she seemed to regard him in the light of a young cock, who, having crowed lustily once or twice at early dawn, has strained his neck to such a pitch that he can only emit hoarse, feeble, gurgling sounds after that.

Moreover, I almost felt sorry for that woman; and I thought, if I were only in her place, how disappointed I should be. And I sighed, repeating almost audibly,—'Were I but in her stead.'

The image which had formed itself within my mind so vividly was all at once reverberated within René's brain; and he thought, if instead of this lady's mouth those lips were my lips; and his phallus at once stiffened and awoke into life; the glands swelled with blood; not only an erection took place, but it almost ejaculated. The Countess—for she was a Countess—was herself surprised at this sudden change, and stopped, for she had now obtained what she wanted; and she knew that—'*Dépasser le but, c'est manquer la chose.*'

Teleny, however, began to fear that if he had his mistress' face before his eyes, my image might entirely vanish; and that—beautiful as she was—he would never be able to accomplish his work to the end. So he began by covering her with kisses; then deftly turned her on her belly. She yielded without understanding what was required of her. He bent her pliant body on her knees, so that she presented a most beautiful sight to his view.

This splendid sight ravished him to such an extent that by looking at it his hitherto limp tool acquired its full size and stiffness, and in its lusty vigor leapt in such a way that it knocked against his navel.

He was even tempted for a moment to introduce it within the small dot of a hole, which, if not exactly the den of life, is surely that of pleasure; but he forbore. He even resisted the temptation of kissing it, or of darting his tongue into it; but bending over her, and placing himself between her legs, he tried to introduce the glans within the aperture of her two lips, now thick and swollen by dint of much rubbing.

Wide apart as her legs were, he first had to open the lips with his fingers on account of the mass of bushy hair that grew all around them; for now the tiny curls had entangled themselves together like tendrils, as if to bar the entrance; therefore, when he had brushed the hair aside, he pressed his tool in it, but the turgid dry flesh arrested him. The clitoris thus pressed danced with delight, so that he took it in his hand, and rubbed and shook it softly and gently on the top part of her lips.

She began to shake, to rub herself with delight; she groaned, she sobbed hysterically; and when he felt himself bathed with delicious tears he thrust his instrument far within her body, clasping her tightly around the neck. So, after a few bold strokes, he managed to get in the whole of the rod down to the very root of the column, crushing his hair against hers, so far in the utmost recesses of the womb that it gave her a pleasurable pain as it touched the neck of the vagina.

For about ten minutes—which to her felt an eternity—she continued panting, throbbing, gasping, groaning, shrieking, roaring, laughing, and crying in the vehemence of her delight.

'Oh! Oh! I am feeling it again! In—in—quick —quicker! There! there!—enough!—stop!'

But he did not listen to her, and he went on plunging and re-plunging with increasing vigor. Having vainly begged for a truce, she began to move again with renewed life.

Having her *a retro*, his thoughts were thus concentrated upon me; and the tightness of the orifice in which the penis was sheathed, added to the titillation produced by the lips of the womb, gave him such an overpowering sensation that he redoubled his strength, and shoved his muscular instrument with such mighty strokes that the frail woman shook under the repeated thumps. Her knees were almost giving way under the brutal force he displayed. When again, all at once, the flood-gates of the seminal ducts were open, and he squirted a jet of molten liquid down into the innermost recesses of her womb.

A moment of delirium followed; the contraction of all her muscles gripped him and sucked him up eagerly, greedily; and after a short spasmodic convulsion, they both fell senseless side by side, still tightly wedged against one another.

—And so ends the Epistle!

—Not quite so, for nine months afterwards the Countess gave birth to a fine boy—

—Who, of course, looked like his father. Doesn't every child look like its father?

—Still, this one happened to look neither like the Count nor like Teleny.

—Who the deuce did it look like then?

—Like myself. The boy looked like me.

—Bosh!

—Bosh as much as you like. Anyhow, the rickety old Count is very proud of this son of his, having discovered a certain likeness between his only heir and the portrait of one of his ancestors. He is always pointing out this atavism to all his visitors; but whenever he struts about, and begins to expound learnedly over the matter, I am told that the Countess shrugs her shoulders and puckers down her lips contemptuously, as if she were not quite convinced of the fact.

5

You have not told me when you met Teleny,
or how your meeting was brought about.

—Just have a little patience, and you will
know all. You can understand that after I had
seen the Countess leave his house at dawn, bearing on her face the expression of the emotions
she had felt, I was anxious to get rid of my
criminal infatuation.

At times I even persuaded myself that I did
not care for René any more. Only when I
thought that all my love had vanished, he had
but to look at me, and I felt it gush back strong-

er than ever, filling my heart and bereaving me of my reason.

I could find no rest either night or day.

I thereupon made up my mind not to see Teleny again, not to attend any of his concerts; but lovers' resolutions are like April showers, and at the last minute the slightest excuse was good enough to make me waver and change my decision.

I was, moreover, curious and anxious to know if the Countess or anybody else would go to meet him again, and pass the night with him.

—Well, and were these visits repeated?

—No, the Count returned unexpectedly; and then both he and the Countess started for Nice.

A short time afterwards, however, as I was always on the watch, I saw Teleny leave the theatre with Briancourt.

There was nothing strange in that. They walked arm-in-arm, and wended their way towards Teleny's lodgings.

I lingered behind, following them step by step at some distance. I had been jealous of the Countess; I was ten times more so of Briancourt.

'If he is going to pass every night with a new bed-fellow,' said I to myself, 'why did he tell me that his heart was yearning for mine?'

And still, within my soul I felt sure that he loved me; that all these other loves were caprices; that his feelings for me were something more than the pleasure of the senses; that it was real, heart-sprung, genuine love.

Having reached the door of Teleny's house, both the young men stopped and began to talk.

The street was a solitary one. Only some belated homegoers were every now and then to be seen, trudging sleepily onward. I had stopped at the corner of the street, pretending to read an advertisement, but in reality to follow the movements of the two young men.

All at once I thought they were about to part, for I saw Briancourt stretch out both his hands and grasp Teleny's. I shivered with gladness. After all, I have wronged Briancourt, was the thought that came into my mind; must every man and woman be in love with the pianist?

My joy, however, was not of long duration, for Briancourt had pulled Teleny towards him, and their lips met in a long kiss, a kiss which for me was gall and wormwood; then, after a few words, the door of Teleny's house was opened and the two young men went in.

When I had seen them disappear, tears of rage, of anguish, of disappointment started from my eyes, I ground my teeth, I bit my lips to the blood, I stamped my feet, I ran on like a madman, I stopped for a moment before the closed door, and vented my anger in thumping the feelingless wood. At last, hearing footsteps approaching, I went on. I walked about the streets for half the night, then fagged out mentally and bodily, I returned home at early dawn.

—And your mother?

—My mother was not in town just then, she was at—, where I shall tell you her adventures some other time, for I can assure you they are worth hearing.

On the morrow, I took a firm resolution not to go to Teleny's concerts any more, not to follow him about, but to forget him entirely. I should have left town, but I thought I had found out another means of getting rid of this horrible infatuation.

Our chambermaid having lately got married, my mother had taken into her service—for reasons best known to herself—a country wench of sixteen or thereabouts, but who, strange to say, looked far younger than she really was, for as a rule those village girls look far older than their years. Although I did not find her good looking, still, everybody seemed smitten by her charms. I cannot say she had anything rustic or countrified about her, for that would awake at once in your mind a vague idea of something awkward or ungainly, while she was as pert as a sparrow, and as graceful as a kitten; still, she had a strong country freshness—nay, I might almost say, tartness—about her like that of a strawberry or a raspberry that grows in mossy thickets.

Seeing her in her town-dress you always fancied you had once met her in picturesque rags, with a bit of red kerchief on her shoulders, and with the savage grace of a young doe standing under leafy boughs, surrounded by eglantine and briers, ready to dart off at the slightest sound.

She had the slender lithesomeness of a young

boy, and might well have been taken for one, had it not been for the budding, round, and firm breasts, that swelled out her dress.

Although she seemed slyly conscious that not one of her movements was lost on the bystanders, still she not only seemed heedless of anyone's admiration, but was even quite vexed if it were expressed either by words or by signs.

Woe to the poor fellow who could not keep his feelings within bounds; she soon made him feel that if she had the beauty and freshness of the dog-rose, she also had its sharp thorns.

Of all the men she had ever known, I was the only one that had never taken the slightest notice of her. For my part, she simply—like all women—left me perfectly indifferent. I was therefore the only man she liked. Her cat-like grace, however, her slightly hoydenish ways, which gave her the appearance of a Ganymede, pleased me, and although I knew very well that I felt no love nor even the slightest attraction for her, still I believed that I might learn to like and perhaps be fond of her. Could I but have felt some sensuality towards her, I think I would even have gone so far as to marry her, rather than become a sodomite, and have an unfaithful man who did not care for me, as my lover.

Anyhow, I asked myself, might I not feel some slight pleasure with her, just enough to quiet my senses, to lull my maddened brain to rest?

And yet which was the greater evil of the two, the one of seducing a poor girl to ruin her, and making her the mother of a poor unhappy child, or that of yielding to the passion which was shattering my body and my mind?

Our honorable society winks at the first peccadillo, and shudders with horror at the second, and as our society is composed of honorable men, I suppose the honorable men which make up our virtuous society are right.

What private reasons they have to make them think in this way, I really do not know.

In the exasperated state in which I was, life was intolerable, I could not bear it any longer.

Weary and worn out by a sleepless night, with my blood parched by excitement and by absinthe, I returned home, took a cold bath, dressed, and called the girl into my room.

When she saw my jaded look, my pale face, my hollow eyes, she stared at me, then—

'Are you ill, sir?' she asked.

'Yes; I am not well.'

'And where were you last night?'

'Where?' I asked scornfully.

'Yes; you did not come home,' said she, defiantly.

I answered her with a nervous laugh.

I understood that a nature like hers had to be mastered all of a sudden rather than tamed by degrees. I therefore caught her within my arms and pressed my lips upon hers. She tried to free herself, but rather like a defenseless bird fluttering with its wings than like a cat thrusting out its claws from inside its velvet paws.

She writhed within my arms, rubbing her

breasts against my chest, her thighs against my legs. Nevertheless, I kept her crushed against my body, kissing her mouth, pressing my burning lips against her own, breathing her fresh and healthy breath.

It was the first time she had ever been kissed on her mouth, and, as she told me afterwards, the sensation shook her whole frame like a strong electric current.

I saw, in fact, that her head was reeling, and her eyes swimming with the emotion which my kisses produced on her nervous constitution.

When I wanted to thrust my tongue into her mouth, her maidenly coyness revolted; she resisted and would not have it. It seemed, said she, as if a piece of burning iron had been thrust into her mouth, and it made her feel as though she were committing a most heinous crime. .

'No, no,' cried she, 'you are smothering me. You are killing me, leave me, I cannot breathe, leave me or I'll call for help.'

But I persisted and soon my tongue down to its very root was in her mouth. I then lifted her up in my arms, for she was as light as a feather, and I stretched her upon the bed. There the fluttering bird was no longer a defenseless dove, but rather a falcon with claws and sharp beak, struggling with might and main, scratching and biting my hands, threatening to pull out my eyes, thumping me with all her strength.

Nothing is a greater incentive to pleasure than a fight. A short tussle with some tingling slaps and a few cuffs will set any man aglow, while a sound flagellation will rouse the blood of the most sluggish old man, better than any aphrodisiac.

The struggle excited her as much as it did me, and yet no sooner had I stretched her down, than she managed forthwith to roll down all in a bundle on the floor; but I was up to her tricks and over her. She managed, however, to slip like an eel from under me, and with a bound like a young kid, made for the door. I had, however, locked it.

A new scuffle ensued, I was now bent upon having her. Had she yielded tamely, I should have ordered her out of the room, but resistance rendered her desirable.

I clasped her within my arms, she writhed and sighed, and every part of our bodies came into strong contact. Then I thrust my leg between hers, our arms were entwined and her breasts were palpitating against my chest. During all this time she belabored me with blows, and each one as it fell seemed to set both her blood and mine on fire.

I had thrown off my coat. The buttons of my waistcoat and trousers were all giving way, my shirt-collar had been torn off, my shirt was soon in rags, my arms were bleeding in several places. Her eyes were glistening like those of a lynx, her lips were pouted with lust, she now seemed to struggle not to defend her maidenhood, but rather for the pleasure the fight gave her.

As I pressed my mouth on hers, I felt her whole body quiver with delight, nay once— and once only — I felt the tip of her tongue thrust slightly within my mouth, and then she seemed maddened with pleasure. She was in fact like a young Maenad in her first initiation.

I actually began to desire her, and yet I felt sorry to sacrifice her at once on love's altar, for this little game was worth being rehearsed more than once.

I lifted her again in my arms and put her on the bed.

How pretty she looked as I held her down. Her curly and wavy hair dishevelled by the fight was strewn in locks all over the pillows. Her dark lively eyes, with their short but thick lashes were twinkling with an almost phosphorescent fire, her face all aglow, was bedabbled with my blood, her parted, panting lips would have made the soft phallus of some old worn-out *monsignore* leap with renewed life.

I had pinioned her down and for a moment stood over her, admiring her. My glances seemed to irritate her, and she struggled once more to be free.

The hooks and eyes of her dress had given way, so that there was just a glimpse of fair flesh, gilt by many a glowing harvest sun, and of two swelling breasts, to be seen; and you know how much more exciting this glimpse is than the wanton display of all the flesh exhibited at balls, theatres, and brothels.

I tore away all obstacles. I thrust one hand

into her bosom, and I tried to slip the other one under her dress; but her skirts were so tightly twisted between her legs, and these were so firmly entwined together, that there was no getting them apart.

After many stifled cries, that seemed more like the twittering of some wounded bird, after much tugging and tearing on my side, scratching and biting on hers, my hand finally reached her naked knees; then it slipped up to the thighs. She was not stout, but as firm and as muscular as an acrobat. My hand reached the parting of the two legs; finally, I felt the slight down that covers Venus' mount.

It was useless to try and thrust my forefinger between the lips. I rubbed her a little. She screamed for mercy. The lips parted slightly. I tried to get my finger in.

'You are hurting me; you are scratching me,' she cried.

Finally her legs relaxed, her dress was up, and she burst into tears—tears of fear, shame, and vexation!

My finger then stopped; and as I withdrew it I felt that it was also wet with tears—tears which were by no means briny ones.

'Come, don't be frightened!' said I, taking her head between my hands, and kissing her repeatedly. 'I was only joking. I do not mean to harm you. There, you can get up! You can go, if you like. I surely will not detain you against your free will.'

And thereupon I thrust my hand within her

bosom, and began to pinch the tiny nipple, in size no bigger than a luscious wild strawberry, of which she seemed to have all the fragrance. She shook with excitement and delight as I did so.

'No,' she said, without attempting to get up, 'I am in your power. You can do with me what you like. I can't help myself any longer. Only remember, if you ruin me, I shall kill myself.'

There was such an earnestness in her eyes as she said this that I shivered, and let her go. Could I ever forgive myself, if I were the cause of her committing self murder?

And still the poor girl looked at me with such loving, longing eyes, that it was plain she was unable to bear the scathing fire that consumed her. Was it not my duty, then, to make her feel that soothing ecstasy of bliss she evidently longed to taste?

'I swear to you,' said I, 'that I shall do you no harm; so do not be afraid, only keep quiet.'

I pulled up her thick linen chemise, and I perceived the tiniest slit that could be seen, with two lips of a coralline hue, shaded by a soft, silky, black down. They had the color, the gloss, the freshness of those pink shells so plentiful on Eastern strands.

Leda's charms, which made Jupiter turn into a swan, or Danae's, when she opened her thighs to receive far into her womb the burning golden shower, could not have been more tempting than the lips of this young girl.

They parted of their own inward life, displaying, as they did so, a tiny berry, fresh with healthy life—a drop of dew incarnadined within the crimson petals of a budding rose.

My tongue pressed it closely for a second, and the girl was madly convulsed with that burning pleasure she had never dreamt of before. A moment afterwards we were again in each other's arms.

'Oh, Camille,' she said, 'you do not know how I love you!'

She waited for an answer. I closed her mouth with a kiss.

'But tell me. Do you love me? Can you love me only a little?'

'Yes,' said I, faintly; for even in such a moment I could not bring myself to tell a lie.

She looked at me for a second.

'No, you don't.'

'Why not?'

'I don't know. I feel that you do not care a straw for me. Tell me, is it not so?'

'Well, if you think so, how can I convince you to the contrary?'

'I don't ask you to marry me. I would not be any man's kept mistress, but if you really love me—'

She did not finish her phrase.

'Well!'

'Can you not understand?' she said, hiding her face behind my ear, and nestling closer to me.

'No.'

'Well, if you love me, I am yours.'

What was I to do? I felt loath to have a girl who offered herself so unconditionally, and yet would it not have been more than foolish to let her go without satisfying her craving and my own desire?

—And then you know as for committing suicide it's all nonsense.

—Not quite so much as you think.

—Well, well, what did you do?

—I? Well, I went halfway.

Kissing her, I laid her on her side, I opened the tiny lips, I pressed the tip of my phallus between them. They parted, and little by little, half of the glans, then the whole head, went in.

I pushed gently, but it seemed caught on each side, and especially in front it found an almost insurmountable obstacle. Just as when driving a nail in a wall, the point meets a stone, and hammering away, the tip gets blunt, then turns on itself, so as I pressed harder, the point of my tool was crushed and strangled. I wriggled to find a way out of this blind alley.

She groaned, but more with pain than with pleasure. I groped my way in the dark and gave another thrust, but my battering ram only crushed its head the more against the stronghold. I was in doubt whether I had not better put her on her back and force my entrance in real battle array, but as I pulled back I felt that I was almost overcome—no, not almost—but quite so, for I squirted her all over with my creamy, life-giving fluid. She, poor thing, felt nothing, or very little, while I, unnerved as I had been till then, and exhausted by my nightly rambles, fell almost senseless by her side. She looked at me for a moment, then sprang up like a cat, caught up the key that had fallen out of my pocket, and with a bound—was out of the door.

Being too jaded to follow her, I was, a few moments afterwards, fast asleep; the first sound rest I had had for a long time.

For a few days I was somewhat quieted, I even gave up attending the concerts and haunts where I could see René; I almost began to think that in time I might get indifferent, and forget him.

I was too eager, I endeavored so hard to blot him at once from my mind, that my very anxiety prevented me from succeeding in doing so; I was so frightened not to be able to forget him, that that fear itself always brought his image to my mind.

—And your girl?

—If I am not mistaken she felt for me what I felt for Teleny. She deemed it her bounden duty to avoid me, she even tried to despise me, to hate me, but she could not succeed in doing so.

—But why to hate you?

—She seemed to understand that if she was still a virgin, it was simply because I cared so little for her; I had felt some pleasure with her, and that was more than enough for me.

Had I loved and deflowered her, she would

only have loved me more tenderly for the wound I had inflicted upon her.

When I asked her if she was not grateful to me for having respected her maidenhood, she simply answered, 'No!' and it was a very decided 'no' indeed. 'Besides,' she added, 'you did nothing, simply because you could do nothing.'

'I could not?'

'No.'

A scuffle ensued again. She was once more locked within my arms and we were wrestling like two prize fighters, with as much eagerness though surely with less skill. She was a muscular little vixen, by no means weak; moreover she had begun to understand the zest which fighting gives to the victory.

It was a real pleasure to feel her body palpitating against mine; and though she was longing to yield, it was only after much ado that I could get my mouth on hers.

With no little difficulty I put her on my bed, and managed to get my head under her skirts.

Women are silly creatures, full of absurd prejudices; and this unsophisticated country wench considered the compliment I was about to pay to her sexual organ as something like buggery.

She called me a dirty beast, a pig, and other such pleasing epithets. She began by writhing and wriggling, and trying to slip away from me, but she thus only added to the pleasure I was giving her.

Finally, she wedged my head between her thighs and pressed the nape of my neck with both her hands, so that even if I had wanted to take my tongue away from her burning lips, I could only have done so with an effort.

I, however, remained there, darting, licking, scraping the little clitoris, till it cried for mercy, and its tears convinced her that this was a pleasure not to be disdained, for this I have found is the only argument with which to convince a woman.

When all the inner parts were thoroughly lubricated by my tongue, and moistened by the soothing overflowings of unbearable pleasure; when she had tasted that ecstatic joy which one virgin can give to another without inflicting any pain or breaking the seal of her innocence, then the sight of her rapture made my own cock crow lustily. I therefore let it out of its dim dungeon, to drive it into the dark den.

My acorn went in merrily, and then it was stopped in its career. Another mighty thrust gave me more pain than pleasure, for the ro sistance was so great that my ramrod seemed sprained in the action; the narrow and firm walls of the vagina dilated, and my piston was jammed in as though in a tight glove, and yet the hymeneal tissue was not reached.

I asked myself why foolish nature has thus barred the way of pleasure? Is it to make the vainglorious bridegroom believe that he is the pioneer of the unexplored regions, but does he not know that midwives are always artfully repairing the locks that adulterine keys have opened? Is it to make a religious ceremony out of it, and to give the plucking of this bud to some father confessor, this having long been among the many prerequisites of the priest-craft?

The poor girl felt as if a knife were being plunged within her, still she did not scream, nor moan, although her eyes filled with tears.

Another thrust, one more effort, and the veil of the temple would be rent in twain.

I stopped in time, however.

'Can I, or can I not have you?'

'You have ruined me already,' she replied quietly.

'I have not; you are still a virgin, simply because I am not a rascal. Only tell me, can I have you or not?'

'If you love me, you can have me, but if you only do so for a moment's pleasure . . . still, do what you like, but I swear that I'll kill myself afterwards, if you don't care for me.'

'These are things that are said and not done.'

'You'll see.'

I pulled my phallus out of the den, but before allowing her to rise, I tickled her gently with the tip, making her feel ample satisfaction for the pain I had inflicted on her.

'Could I or could I not have had you?' said I.

'Imbecile,' she hissed like a snake, as she slipped out of my arms and was beyond my reach.

'Wait till next time, and you will then see who is the imbecile,' said I, but she was already out of hearing.

—I must own you were somewhat of a green-horn; I suppose, however, that you had your revenge, next time.

—My revenge, if it can be called by that name, was a fearful one.

Our coachman, a young, stalwart, broad-shouldered and brawny fellow, whose fondness had hitherto expended itself on his horses, had fallen in love with this girl, who looked as sapless as a holly twig.

He had tried to woo her in honorable fashion in every possible way. His former continence and his newly-born passion had softened all that was boorish in him, he had plied her with flowers, ribbons and trinkets, but she had scorn-fully refused all his presents.

He had offered to marry her at once; he had gone so far as to make her a free gift of a cottage and a bit of land he possessed in his country.

She exasperated him by treating him almost with scorn, resenting his love as an insult. An irresistible longing was in his eyes, in hers a vacant stare.

Goaded to madness by her indifference, he had tried by strength what he could not obtain by love, and had had to understand that the fairer sex is not always the weaker one.

After his attempt and failure she tantalized him all the more. Whenever she met him she would put her thumbnail up to her top teeth and emit a slight sound.

The cook, who had a latent fondness for this

strong and sinewy young fellow, and who must have had an inkling that something had taken place between this girl and myself, evidently informed him of the fact, arousing thereby in him an ungovernable fit of jealousy.

Stung to the quick, he hardly knew whether he loved or hated this girl most, and he cared but little what became of him provided he could satisfy his craving for her. All the softness which love had awakened gave way to the sexual energy of the male.

Unperceived, or probably let in by the cook, he stealthily secreted himself in her room, and ensconced himself behind an old screen, which, together with other lumber, had been stowed away there.

His intention was to remain hidden till she was fast asleep, and then to get into her bed, and, *nolens volens,* to pass the night with her.

After waiting there some time in mortal anxiety—for every minute was like an hour to him—he finally saw her come in.

As she did so, she shut and locked the door behind her. His whole frame shook with joy at that slight act. First she clearly did not expect anyone, then she was in his possession.

Two holes which he had made in the paper of the screen enabled him to see everything perfectly. Little by little she prepared herself for the night. She undid her hair, then did it up again in a loose knot. After which she took off her dress, her stays, her skirts, and all her undergarments. At last she was in her chemise.

She then, with a deep sigh, took a rosary, and began to pray. He himself was a religious man, and would fain have repeated his prayers after her, but he vainly tried to mumble a few words. All his thoughts were on her.

The moon was now in its full, and flooded the room with its mellow light, falling on her naked arms, on her rounded shoulders and small protruding breasts, shedding upon them all kinds of opaline tints, giving them the delicate gloss of satin and the sheen of amber, while the linen chemise fell in folds on her nether parts with the softness of flannel.

He remained there motionless, almost awe-stricken, with his eyes fastened upon her, holding his thick, feverish breath, gloating on her with that fixed eagerness with which the cat watches the mouse, or the hunter the game. All the powers of his body seemed concentrated in the sense of vision.

At last she finished her prayers, crossed herself, and rose. She lifted her right foot to get into her rather high bed, showing the coachman her slender though well-shaped legs, her small but rounded buttocks, and, as she bent forward, the nether part of the two lips gaped, as one knee was already on the bed.

The coachman, however, had not time enough to see this, for with a cat-like bound he was already on her.

She uttered the faintest of cries, but he had already clasped her in his arms.

'Leave me! leave me! or I'll call for help.'

'Call as much as you like, darling; but no one can or will come to your aid before I have had you, for I swear by the Virgin Mary that I'll not leave this room before I've enjoyed you. If that *bougre* can use you for his pleasure, so shall I. If he has not—well, after all it is better to be a poor man's wife than a rich man's whore; and you know whether I have been wanting to marry you or not.'

Saying these words, holding her with one hand clasped as in a vise, her back against him, he tried with the other to twist her head round so as to get to her lips; but, seeing that he could not, he pressed her down on the bed. Holding her by the nape of the neck, he thrust his other hand between her legs and gripped her middle parts in his brawny palm.

Being ready beforehand, thrusting himself between her parted legs, he began to press his instrument against the lower part of the half-opened lips.

Swollen and dry as they had remained after my attempt, his good-sized turgid phallus slipped, and the tip lodged itself at the upper corner. Then, like a heavy laden stamen when kissed by the deflowering wind scatters its pollen on the open ovaries around it, so, hardly had the turgid and overflowing phallus touched the tiny clitoris when it jutted forth its sappy seed not only on it, but it squirted over all the surrounding parts. As she felt her stomach and thighs bathed by the warm fluid, it seemed to her that she was burnt by some scalding corrosive poison, and she writhed as if in pain.

But the more she struggled, the greater was the pleasure he felt, and his groans and the gurgling that seemed to mount from his middle parts up to his throat, testified to the rapture in which he was. He rested for a moment but his organ lost none of its strength or stiffness, her contortions only excited him the more. Putting his huge hand between her legs, he uplifted her on the bed, higher than she was, and brutally holding her down, he pressed the fleshy extremity of the glans against her, and the lips bathed in the slimy fluid parted asunder easily.

It was hardly a question with him now of pleasure given or received, it was the wild overpowering eagerness which the male brute displays in possessing the female, for you might have killed him, but he would not have let go his hold. He thrust at her with all the mighty heaviness of a bull; with another effort, the glans was lodged between the lips, another one more, half the column was already in, when it was stopped by the as yet unperforated but highly dilated virginal membrane. Feeling himself thus stopped at the outer orifice of the vagina he felt a moment of exultation.

He kissed her head with rapture.

'You are mine,' he cried with joy; 'mine for life and death, mine for ever and ever.'

She evidently must have compared his wild delight with my cold indifference, and yet she tried to scream, but his hand stopped her mouth. She bit him, still he did not heed it.

Then, regardless of the pain he was causing, heedless of the strain he was giving the prisoner lodged in its narrow cage, he clasped her with all his strength, and with a last powerful thrust the vulva was not only reached but crossed; the membrane—so strong in the poor girl— was slit, his Priapus was lodged deep into the vagina, and it slid up to the neck of the womb.

She uttered a loud, shrill, piercing cry of pain and anguish, and the scream vibrating through the stillness of the night was heard all over the house. Regardless of any consequences of the noises already heard in answer to the scream, regardless of the blood gushing forth, he rapturously plunged and re-plunged his lance in the wound he had made, and his groans of pleasure were mixed with her plaintive wail.

Finally he pulled his limber weapon out of her; she was free, but senseless and faint.

I was just upon the steps, when I heard the cry. Although I was not thinking of the poor girl, still, at once it seemed to me as if I recognized her voice, I flew up the steps, I rushed into the house, and I found the cook pale and trembling in the passage.

'Where is Catherine?'

'In her room—I—I think.'

'Then, who screamed?'

'But—but I don't know. Perhaps she did.'

'And why don't you go to help her?'

'The door is locked,' said she, looking aghast.

I rushed to the door. I shook it with all my strength.

'Catherine, open! What's the matter?'

At the sound of my voice the poor girl came back to life.

With another mighty shake I burst the lock. The door opened.

I had just time enough to catch sight of the girl in her blood-stained chemise.

Her loose hair was all dishevelled. Her eyes were gleaming with a wild fire. Her face was contorted by pain, shame, and madness. She looked like Cassandra after she had been violated by Ajax's soldiers.

As she stood, not far from the window, her glances from the coachman fell upon me with loathing and scorn.

She now knew what the love of men was. She rushed to the casement. I bounded towards her, but forestalling me, she leapt out before the coachman or myself could prevent her; and although I caught the end of her garment, her weight tore it, and I was left with a rag in my hand.

We heard a heavy thud, a scream, a few groans, then silence.

The girl had been true to her word.

This shocking suicide of our maid absorbed
all my thoughts for a few days, and gave me
no slight amount of trouble and worry for some
time afterwards.

Besides, as I was no casuist, I asked myself
whether I had not had some share in prompting
her to commit such a rash act; I therefore tried
to make amends to the coachman, at least, by
helping him as much as I could out of his trouble. Moreover, if I had not been fond of the

girl, I had really tried to love her, so that I was greatly upset by her death.

My manager, who was far more my master than I was his, seeing the shattered state of my nerves, persuaded me to undertake a short business journey, which otherwise he would have had to make himself.

All these circumstances obliged me to keep my thoughts away from Teleny, who had lately engrossed them so entirely. I therefore tried to come to the conclusion that I had quite forgotten him; and I was already congratulating myself on having mastered a passion that had rendered me contemptible in my own eyes.

On my return home I not only shunned him, but I even avoided reading his name in the papers—nay, whenever I saw it on the bills in the street, I turned my head away from it, notwithstanding all the attraction it had for me; such was the fear I had of falling under his magic spell. And yet, was it possible for me to continue avoiding him? Would not the slightest accident bring us together again? And then—?

I tried to believe that the power he had over me had vanished, and that it was not possible for him to acquire it again. Then, to make doubly sure, I resolved to cut him dead the first time we met. Moreover I was in hopes he would leave the town—for some time at least, if not forever.

Not long after my return, I was with my mother in a box at the theatre, when all at once the door opened and Teleny appeared in the doorway.

On seeing him I felt myself grow pale and then red, my knees seemed to be giving way, my heart began to beat with such mighty thumps that my breast was ready to burst. For a moment, I felt all my good resolutions give way; then, loathing myself for being so weak, I snatched up my hat, and—scarcely bowing to the young man—I rushed out of the box like a madman, leaving my mother to apologize for my strange behavior. No sooner was I out than I felt drawn back, and I almost returned to beg his forgiveness. Shame alone prevented me from doing so.

When I re-entered the box, my mother, vexed and astonished, asked me what had made me act in such a boorish way to the musician, whom everybody welcomed and made much of.

'Two months ago, if I remember rightly,' said she, 'there was hardly another pianist like him; and now, because the press has turned against him, he is even below being bowed to.'

'The press is against him? said I, with up-lifted eyebrows.

'What! have you not read how bitterly he has been criticized of late?'

'No, I have had other matters to think about than pianists.'

'Well, of late he seems to have been out of sorts. His name has appeared on the bills several times, and then he has not played; while at the last concerts he went through his pieces in a most humdrum, lifeless way, so very different from his former brilliant execution.'

I felt as if a hand was gripping at my heart within my breast, still I tried to keep my features as indifferent as possible.

'I am sorry for him,' I said, listlessly; 'but then, I daresay the ladies will console him for the taunts of the press, and thus blunt the points of their arrows.'

My mother shrugged her shoulders and drew down the corners of her lips disdainfully. She little guessed either my thoughts, or how bitterly I regretted the way in which I had acted towards the young man whom — well, it was useless to mince matters any longer, or to give myself the lie—I still loved. Yes, loved more than ever — loved to distraction.

On the morrow, I looked for all the papers in which his name was mentioned, and I found— it may perhaps be vanity on my part to think so—that from the very day I had ceased to attend his concerts, he had been playing wretchedly, until at last his critics, once so lenient, had all joined against him, endeavoring to bring him to a better sense of the duty he owed to his art, to the public, and to himself.

About a week afterwards, I again went to hear him play.

As he came in, I was surprised to see the change wrought in him in that short space of time; he was not only careworn and dejected, but pale, thin, and sickly-looking. He seemed, in fact, to have grown ten years older in those few days. There was in him that alteration which my mother had noticed in me on her return from Italy; but she, of course, had attributed it to the shock my nerves had just received.

As he came on, some few persons tried to cheer him by clapping their hands, but a low murmur of disapproval, followed by a slight hissing sound, stopped these feeble attempts at once. He seemed scornfully indifferent to both sounds. He sat listlessly down, like a person worn out by fever, but, as one of the musical reporters stated, the fire of art began all at once to glow within his eyes. He cast a sidelong glance on the audience, a searching look full of love and of thankfulness.

Then he began to play, not as if his task were a weary one, but as if he were pouring out his heavily-laden soul; and the music sounded like the warbling of a bird which, in its attempt to captivate its mate, pants forth its flood of rapture, resolved either to conquer or to die in profused strains of unpremeditated art.

It is needless to say that I was thoroughly overcome, while the whole crowd was thrilled by the sweet sadness of his song.

The piece finished, I hurried out—frankly, in the hope of meeting him. While he had been playing, a mighty struggle had been going on within myself—between my heart and my brain; and the glowing senses asked cold reason, what was the use of fighting against an ungovernable passion? I was, indeed, ready to forgive him for all I had suffered, for after all, had I any right to be angry with him?

As I entered the room he was the first— nay, the only person I saw. A feeling of indescribable delight filled my whole being, and my heart seemed to bound forth towards him. All at once, however, all my rapture passed away, my blood froze in my veins, and love gave way to anger and hatred. He was arm-in-arm with Briancourt, who, openly congratulating him on his success, was evidently clinging to him like the ivy to the oak. Briancourt's eyes and mine met; in his there was a look of exultation; in mine, of withering scorn.

As soon as Teleny saw me, he at once broke loose from Briancourt's clutches, and came up to me. Jealousy maddened me, I gave him the stiffest and most distant of bows and passed on, utterly disregarding his outstretched hands.

I heard a slight murmur amongst the bystanders, and as I walked away I saw with the corner of my eye his hurt look, his blushes that came and went, and his expression of wounded pride. Though hot-tempered, he bowed resignedly, as if to say: 'Be it as you will,' and he went back to Briancourt, whose face was beaming with satisfaction.

Briancourt said, 'He has always been a cad, a tradesman, a proud *parvenu!*' just loud enough for the words to reach my ear. 'Do not mind him.'

'No,' added Teleny, musingly, 'it is I who am to blame, not he.'

Little did he understand with what a bleeding heart I walked out of the room, yearning at every step to turn back, and to throw my arms around his neck before everybody, and beg his forgiveness.

I wavered for a moment, whether to go and offer him my hand or not. Alas! do we often yield to the warm impulse of the heart? Are we not, instead, always guided by the advice of the calculating, conscience-muddled, clay-cold brain?

It was early, yet I waited for some time in the street, watching for Teleny to come out. I had made up my mind that if he was alone, I would go and beg his pardon for my rudeness.

After a short time, I saw him appear at the door with Briancourt.

My jealousy was at once rekindled, I turned on my heels and walked off. I did not want to see him again. On the morrow I would take the first train and go—anywhere, out of the world if I could.

This state of feeling did not last long; and my rage being somewhat subdued, love and curiosity prompted me again to stop. I did so. I looked round; they were nowhere to be seen; still I had wended my steps towards Teleny's house.

I walked back. I glanced down the neighboring streets; they had quite disappeared.

Now that he was lost to sight, my eagerness

to find him increased. They had, perhaps, gone to Briancourt's. I hurried on in the direction of his house.

All at once, I thought I saw two figures like them at a distance. I hastened on like a madman. I lifted up the collar of my coat, I pulled my soft felt hat over my ears, so as not to be recognized, and followed them on the opposite sidewalk.

I was not mistaken. Then they branched off; I after them. Whither were they going in these lonely parts?

So as not to attract their attention I stopped where I saw an advertisement. I slackened, and then quickened my pace. Several times I saw their heads come in close contact, and then Briancourt's arm encircled Teleny's waist.

All this was far worse than gall and wormwood to me. Still, in my misery, I had one consolation; this was to see that, apparently, Teleny was yielding to Briancourt's attentions instead of seeking them.

At last they reached the Quai de—, so busy in the daytime, so lonely at night. There they seemed to be looking for somebody, for they either turned round, scanned the persons they met, or stared at men seated on the benches that are along the quay. I continued following them.

As my thoughts were entirely absorbed, it was some time before I noticed that a man, who had sprung up from somewhere, was walking by my side. I grew nervous; for I fancied that he not only tried to keep pace with me but also to catch my attention, for he hummed and whistled snatches of songs, coughed, cleared his throat, and scraped his feet.

All these sounds fell upon my dreamy ears, but failed to arouse my attention. All my senses were fixed on the two figures in front of me. He therefore walked on, then turned round on his heels, and stared at me. My eyes saw all this without heeding him in the least.

He lingered once more, let me pass, walked on at a brisker pace, and was again beside me. Finally, I looked at him. Though it was cold, he was but slightly dressed. He wore a short, black velvet jacket and a pair of light grey, closely-fitting trousers marking the shape of the thighs and buttocks like tights.

As I looked at him he stared at me again, then smiled with that vacant, vapid, idiotic, facial contraction of a *raccrocheuse*. Then, always looking at me with an inviting leer, he directed his steps towards a neighboring *Vespasienne*.

'What is there so peculiar about me?' I mused, 'that the fellow is ogling me in that way?'

Without turning round, however, or noticing him any further, I walked on, my eyes fixed on Teleny.

As I passed by another bench, someone again scraped his feet and cleared his throat, evidently bent on making me turn my head. I did so.

There was nothing more remarkable about him than there was in the first man I met. Seeing me look at him, he either unbuttoned or buttoned up his trousers.

After a while I again heard steps coming from behind; the person was close up to me. I smelt a strong scent—if the noxious odor of musk or of patchouli can be called a scent.

The person touched me slightly as he passed by. He begged my pardon; it was the man of the velvet jacket, or his Dromio. I looked at him as he again stared at me and grinned. His eyes were painted with khol, his cheeks were dabbed with rouge. He was quite beardless. For a moment, I doubted whether he was a man or a woman; but when he stopped again before the column I was fully persuaded of his sex.

Someone else came with mincing steps, and shaking his buttocks, from behind one of these *pissoirs*. He was an old, wiry, simpering man as shrivelled as a frost-bitten pippin. His cheeks were very hollow, and his projecting cheekbones very red; his face was shaven and shorn, and he wore a wig with long, fair, flaxen locks.

He walked in the posture of the Venus of Medici; that is, with one hand on his middle parts, and the other on his breast. His looks were not only very demure, but there was an almost maidenly coyness about the old man that gave him the appearance of a virgin-pimp.

He did not stare, but cast a sidelong glance at me as he went by. He was met by a workman — a strong and sturdy fellow, either a butcher or a smith by trade. The old man would evidently have slunk by unperceived, but the workman stopped him. I could not hear what they said, for though they were but a few steps away, they spoke in that hushed tone peculiar to lovers; but I seemed to be the object of their talk, for the workman turned and stared at me as I passed. They parted.

The workman walked on for twenty steps, then he turned on his heel and walked back exactly on a line with me, seemingly bent on meeting me face to face.

I looked at him. He was a brawny man, with massive features; clearly, a fine specimen of a male. As he passed by me he clenched his powerful fist, doubled his muscular arm at the elbow, and then moved it vertically hither and thither a few times, like a piston-rod in action, as it slipped in and out of the cylinder.

Some signs are so evidently clear and full of meaning that no initiation is needed to understand them. This workman's sign was one of them.

Now I knew who all these nightwalkers were. Why they so persistently stared at me, and the meaning of all their little tricks to catch my attention. Was I dreaming? I looked around. The workman had stopped, and he repeated his request in a different way. He shut his left fist, then thrust the forefinger of his right hand in the hole made by the palm and fingers, and moved it in and out. He was bluntly explicit.

I was not mistaken. I hastened on, musing whether the cities of the plain had been destroyed by fire and brimstone.

As I learnt later in life, every large city has its particular haunts—its square, its garden for such recreation. And the police? Well, they wink at it, until some crying offense is committed; for it is not safe to stop the mouths of craters. Brothels of men-whores not being allowed, such trysting-places must be tolerated, or the whole is a modern Sodom or Gomorrah.

—What! there are such cities nowadays?

—Aye! for Jehovah has acquired experience with age; so He has got to understand His children a little better than He did of yore, for He has either come to a righter sense of toleration, or, like Pilate, He has washed His hands, and has quite discarded them.

At first I felt a deep sense of disgust at seeing the old catamite pass by me again, and lift, with utmost modesty, his arm from his breast, thrust his bony finger between his lips, and move it in the same fashion as the workman had done his arm, but trying to give all his movements a maidenly coyness. He was— as I learnt later — a *pompeur de dard,* or as I might call him, a 'sperm sucker'; this was his specialty. He did the work for the love of the thing, and an experience of many years had made him a master of his trade. He, it appears, lived in every other respect like a hermit, and only indulged himself in one thing—fine lawn handkerchiefs, either with lace or embroidery, to wipe the amateur's instrument when he had done with it.

The old man went down towards the river's edge, apparently inviting me for a midnight stroll in the mist, under the arches of the bridge, or in some out-of-the-way nook or other corner.

Another man came up from there; this one was adjusting his dress, and scratching his hind parts like an ape. Notwithstanding the creepy feeling these men gave me, the scene was so entirely new that I must say it rather interested me.

—And Teleny?

—I had been so taken up with all these midnight wanderers that I lost sight both of him and of Briancourt, when all at once I saw them reappear.

With them there was a young Zouave sub-lieutenant and a dapper and dashing fellow, and a slim and swarthy youth, apparently an Arab.

The meeting did not seem to have been a carnal one. Anyhow, the soldier was entertaining his friends with his lively talk, and by the few words which my ear caught I understood that the topic was an interesting one. Moreover, as they passed by each bench, the couples seated thereon nudged each other as if they were acquainted with them.

As I passed them I shrugged up my shoulders, and buried my head in my collar. I even put up my handkerchief to my face. Still, notwithstanding all my precautions, Teleny seemed to have recognized me, although I had walked on without taking the slightest notice of him.

I heard their merry laughter as I passed; an echo of loathsome words was still ringing in my ears; sickening faces of effete, womanish men traversed the street, trying to beguile me by all that is nauseous.

I hurried on, sick at heart, disappointed, hating myself and my fellow-creatures, musing whether I was any better than all these worshippers of Priapus who were inured to vice. I was pining for the love of one man who did not care more for me than for any of these sodomites.

It was late at night, and I walked on without exactly knowing where my steps were taking me to. I had not to cross the water on my way home, what then made me do so? Anyhow, all at once I found myself standing in the very middle of the bridge, staring vacantly at the open space in front of me.

The river, like a silvery thoroughfare, parted the town in two. On either side huge shadowy houses rose out of the mist; blurred domes, dim towers, vaporous and gigantic spires stared, quivering, up to the clouds, and faded away in the fog.

Underneath I could perceive the sheen of the cold, bleak, and bickering river, flowing faster and faster, as if fretful at not being able to outdo itself in its own speed, chafing against the arches that stopped it, curling in tiny breakers, and whirling away in angry eddies, while the dark pillars shed patches of ink-black shade on the glittering and shivering stream.

As I looked upon these dancing, restless shadows, I saw a myriad of fiery, snake-like elves gliding to and fro through them, winking and beckoning to me as they twirled and they rolled, luring me down to rest in those Lethean waters.

They were right. Rest must be found below those dark arches, on the soft, slushy sand of that swirling river.

How deep and fathomless those waters seemed! Veiled as they were by the mist, they had all the attraction of the abyss. Why should I not seek there that balm of forgetfulness which alone could ease my aching head, could calm my burning breast?

Why?

Was it because the Almighty had fixed His canon against self-slaughter?

How, when, and where?

With His fiery finger, when He made that *coupe de théatre* on Mount Sinai?

If so, why was He tempting me beyond my strength?

Would any father induce a beloved child to disobey him, simply to have the pleasure of chastising him afterwards? Would any man deflower his own daughter, not out of lust, but only to taunt her with her incontinence? Surely, if such a man ever lived, he was after Jehovah's own image.

No, life is only worth living as long as it is pleasant. To me, just then, it was a burden. The passion I had tried to stifle, and which was merely smouldering, had burst out with renewed strength, entirely mastering me. That crime could therefore only be overcome by another. In my case suicide was not only allowable, but laudable—nay, heroic.

What did the Gospel say? 'If thine eye . . .' and so forth.

All these thoughts whirled through my mind like little fiery snakes. Before me in the mist, Teleny—like a vaporous angel of light—seemed to be quickly gazing at me with his deep, sad, and thoughtful eyes; below, the rushing waters had for me a siren's sweet, enticing voice.

I felt my brain reeling. I was losing my senses. I cursed this beautiful world of ours—this paradise, that man has turned into a hell. I cursed this narrow-minded society of ours, that only thrives upon hypocrisy. I cursed our blighting religion, that lays its veto upon all the pleasures of the senses.

I was already climbing on the parapet, decided to seek forgetfulness in those Stygian waters, when two strong arms clasped me tightly and held me fast.

—It was Teleny?

—It was.

'Camille, my love, my soul, are you mad?' said he, in a stifled, panting voice.

Was I dreaming—was it he? Teleny? Was he

my guardian angel or a tempting demon? Had I gone quite mad?

All these thoughts chased one another, and left me bewildered. Still, after a moment, I understood that I was neither mad nor dreaming. It was Teleny in flesh and blood, for I felt him against me as we were closely clasped in each other's arms. I had wakened to life from a horrible nightmare.

The strain my nerves had undergone, and the utter faintness that followed, together with his powerful embrace, made me feel as if our two bodies clinging closely together had amalgamated or melted into a single one.

A most peculiar sensation came over me at this moment. As my hands wandered over his head, his neck, his shoulders, his arms, I could not feel him at all; in fact, it seemed to me as if I were touching my own body. Our burning foreheads were pressed against each other, and his swollen and throbbing veins seemed my own fluttering pulses.

Instinctively, and without seeking each other, our mouths united by a common consent. We did not kiss, but our breath gave life to our two beings.

I remained vaguely unconscious for some time, feeling my strength ebb slowly away, leaving but vitality enough to know that I was yet alive.

All at once I felt a mighty shock from head to foot; there was a reflux from the heart to the brain. Every nerve in my body was tingling; all my skin seemed pricked with the points of sharp needles. Our mouths which had withdrawn now clung again to each other with newly-awakened lust. Our lips—clearly seeking to graft themselves together—pressed and rubbed with such passionate strength that the blood began to ooze from them—nay, it seemed as if this fluid, rushing up from our two hearts, was bent upon mingling together to celebrate in that auspicious moment the old hymeneal rites of nations—the marriage of two bodies, not by the communion of emblematic wine but of blood itself.

We thus remained for some time in a state of overpowering delirium, feeling every instant, a more rapturous, maddening pleasure in each other's kisses, which kept goading us on to madness by increasing that heat which they could not allay, and by stimulating that hunger they could not appease.

The very quintessence of love was in these kisses. All that was excellent in us—the essential part of our beings—kept rising and evaporating from our lips like the fumes of an ethereal, intoxicating, ambrosial fluid.

Nature, hushed and silent, seemed to hold her breath to look upon us, for such ecstasy of bliss had seldom, if ever, been felt here below. I was subdued, prostrated, shattered. The earth was spinning round me, sinking under my feet. I had no longer strength enough to stand. I felt sick and faint. Was I dying? If so, death must be the happiest moment of our life, for such rapturous joy could never be felt again.

How long did I remain senseless? I cannot tell. All I know is that I awoke in the midst of a whirlwind, hearing the rushing of waters around me. Little by little I came back to consciousness. I tried to free myself from his grasp.

'Leave me! Leave me alone! Why did you not let me die? This world is hateful to me, why should I drag on a life I loathe?'

'Why? For my sake.' Thereupon, he whispered softly, in that unknown tongue of his, some magic words which seemed to sink into my soul. Then he added, 'Nature has formed us for each other; why withstand her? I can only find happiness in your love, and in yours alone; it is not only part of my heart but my soul that pants for yours.'

With an effort of my whole being I pushed him away from me, and staggered back.

'No, no!' I cried, 'do not tempt me beyond my strength; let me rather die.'

'Thy will be done, but we shall die together, so that at least in death we may not be parted. There is an afterlife, we may then, at least, cleave to one another like Dante's Francesca and her lover Paulo. Here,' said he, unwinding a silken scarf that he wore round his waist, 'let us bind ourselves closely together, and leap into the flood.'

I looked at him, and shuddered. So young, so beautiful, and I was thus to murder him! The vision of Antinous as I had seen it the first time he played appeared before me.

He had tied the scarf tightly round his waist, and he was about to pass it around me.

'Come.'

The die was cast. I had not the right to accept such a sacrifice from him.

'No,' said I, 'let us live.'

'Live,' he added, 'and then?'

He did not speak for some moments, as if waiting for a reply to that question which had not been framed in words. In answer to his mute appeal I stretched out my hands towards him. He—as if frightened that I should escape him—hugged me tightly with all the strength of irrepressible desire.

'I love you!' he whispered, 'I love you madly! I cannot live without you any longer.'

'Nor can I,' said I, faintly; 'I have struggled against my passion in vain, and now I yield to it, not tamely, but eagerly, gladly. I am yours, Teleny! Happy to be yours, yours forever and yours alone!'

For all answer there was a stifled hoarse cry from his innermost breast; his eyes were lighted up with a flash of fire; his craving amounted to rage; it was that of the wild beast seizing his prey; that of the lonely male finding at last a mate. Still his intense eagerness was more than that; it was also a soul issuing forth to meet another soul. It was a longing of the senses, and a mad intoxication of the brain.

Could this burning, unquenchable fire that

consumed our bodies be called lust? We clung as hungrily to one another as the famished animal does when it fastens on the food it devours; and as we kissed each other with ever-increasing greed, my fingers were feeling his curly hair, or paddling the soft skin of his neck. Our legs being clasped together, his phallus, in strong erection, was rubbing against mine no less stiff and stark. We were, however, always shifting our position, so as to get every part of our bodies in as close a contact as possible; and thus feeling, clasping, hugging, kissing, and biting each other, we must have looked, on that bridge amidst the thickening fog, like two damned souls suffering eternal torment.

The hand of Time had stopped; and I think we should have continued goading each other in our mad desire until we had quite lost our senses—for we were both on the verge of madness—had we not been stopped by a trifling incident.

A belated cab—wearied with the day's toil—was slowly trudging its way homeward. The driver was sleeping on his box; the poor, broken down jade, with its head drooping almost between its knees, was likewise slumbering — dreaming, perhaps, of unbroken rest, of new-mown hay, of the fresh and flowery pastures of its youth; even the slow rumbling of the wheels had a sleepy, purring, snoring sound in its irksome sameness.

'Come home with me,' said Teleny, in a low,

nervous, and trembling voice; 'come and sleep with me,' added he, in the soft, hushed, and pleading tone of the lover who would fain be understood without words.

I pressed his hands for all answer.

'Will you come?'

'Yes,' I whispered, almost inaudibly.

This low, hardly-articulate sound was the hot breath of vehement desire; this lisped monosyllable was the willing consent to his eagerest wish.

Then he hailed the passing cab, but it was some moments before the driver could be awakened and made to understand what we wanted of him.

As I stepped into the vehicle, my first thought was that in a few minutes Teleny would belong to me. This thought acted upon my nerves as an electric current, making me shive from head to foot.

My lips had to articulate the words, 'Teleny will be mine,' for me to believe it. He seemed to hear the noiseless movement of my lips, for he clasped my head between his hands, and kissed me again and again.

Then, as if feeling a pang of remorse—'You do not repent, do you?' he asked.

'How can I?'

'And you will be mine—mine alone?'

'I never was any other man's nor ever shall be.'

'You will love me forever?'

'And ever.'

'This will be our oath and our act of possession,' he added.

Thereupon he put his arms around me and clasped me to his breast. I entwined my arms round him. By the glimmering, dim light of the cab-lamps I saw his eyes kindle with the fire of madness. His lips—parched with the thirst of his long-suppressed desire, with the pent-up craving of possession—pouted towards mine with a painful expression of dull suffering. We were again sucking up each other's being in a kiss—a kiss more intense, if possible, than the former one. What a kiss that was!

The flesh, the blood, the brain, and that undefined subtler part of our being seemed all to melt together in an ineffable embrace.

A kiss is something more than the first sensual contact of two bodies; it is the breathing forth of two enamored souls.

But a criminal kiss long withstood and fought against, and therefore long yearned after, is beyond this; it is as luscious as forbidden fruit; it is a glowing coal set upon the lips; a fiery brand that burns deep, and changes the blood into molten lead or scalding quicksilver.

Teleny's kiss was really galvanic, for I could taste its sapidity upon my palate. Was an oath needed, when we had given ourselves to one another with such a kiss? An oath is a lip-promise which can be, and is, often forgotten. Such a kiss follows you to the grave.

While our lips clung together, his hand slowly, imperceptibly, unbuttoned my trousers, and stealthily slipped within the aperture, turning every obstacle in its way instinctively aside, then it lay hold of my hard, stiff, and aching phallus which was glowing like a burning coal.

This grasp was as soft as a child's, as expert as a whore's, as strong as a fencer's. He had hardly touched me than I remembered the Countess' words.

Some people, as we all know, are more magnetic than others. Moreover, while some attract, others repel us. Teleny had—for me, at least— a supple, mesmeric, pleasure-giving fluid in his fingers. Nay, the simple contact of his skin thrilled me with delight.

My own hand hesitatingly followed the lead his had given, and I must confess the pleasure I felt in paddling him was really delightful.

Our fingers hardly moved the skin of the penis; but our nerves were so strained, our excitement had reached such a pitch, and the seminal ducts were so full, that we felt them overflowing. There was, for a moment, an intense pain, somewhere about the root of the penis—or rather, within the very core and center of the veins, after which the sap of life began to move slowly, slowly, from within the seminal glands; it mounted up the bulb of the urethra, and up the narrow column, somewhat like mercury within the tube of a thermometer —or rather, like the scalding and scathing lava within the crater of a volcano.

It finally reached the apex; then the slit

gaped, the tiny lips parted, and the pearly creamy, viscous fluid oozed out—not all at once in a gushing jet, but at intervals, and in huge burning tears.

At every drop that escaped out of the body a creepy almost unbearable feeling started from the tips of the fingers, from the ends of the toes, especially from the innermost cells of the brain; the marrow in the spine and within all the bones seemed to melt; and when the different currents—either coursing with the blood or running rapidly up the nervous fibers—met within the phallus (that small instrument made out of muscles and blood-vessels) a tremendous shock took place; a convulsion which annihilated both mind and matter, a quivering delight which everyone has felt, to a greater or lesser degree—often a thrill almost too intense to be pleasurable.

Pressed against each other, all we could do was to try and smother our groans as the fiery drops slowly followed one another.

The prostration which followed the excessive strain of the nerves had set in, when the carriage stopped before the door of Teleny's house —that door at which I had madly struck with my fists a short time before.

We dragged ourselves wearily out of the carriage, but hardly had the portal shut itself upon us than we were again kissing and fondling each other with renewed energy.

After some moments, feeling that our desire was too powerful to be withstood any longer

'Come,' said he, 'why should we linger any longer, and waste precious time here in the darkness and in the cold?'

'Is it dark and is it cold?' was my reply.

He kissed me fondly.

'In the gloom you are my light; in the cold you are my fire; the frozen wastes of the Pole would be a Garden of Eden for me, if you were there,' I continued.

We then groped our way upstairs in the dark, for I would not allow him to light a wax match. I therefore went along, stumbling against him; not that I could not see, but because I was intoxicated with male desire as a drunken man is with wine.

Soon we were in his apartment. When we found ourselves in the small, dimly-lighted antechamber, he opened his arms and stretched them out towards me.

'Welcome!' said he. 'May this home be ever thine.' Then he added, in a low tone, in that unknown, musical tongue, 'My body hungereth for thee, soul of my soul, life of my life!'

He had barely finished these words before we were lovingly caressing each other.

After thus fondling each other for a few moments—'Do you know,' he said, 'that I have been expecting you today?'

'Expecting me?'

'Yes, I knew that sooner or later you would be mine. Moreover, I felt that you would be coming today.'

'How so?'

'I had a presentiment,' he said quite seriously.

'And had I not come?'

'I should have done what you were going to do when I met you, for life without you would have been unbearable.'

'What! drowned yourself?'

'No, not exactly: the river is too cold and bleak, I am too much of a Sybarite for that. No, I should simply have put myself to sleep— the eternal slumber of death, dreaming of you, in this room prepared to receive you, and where no man has ever set his foot.'

Saying these words he opened the door of a small chamber, and ushered me into it. A strong, overpowering smell of white heliotrope first greeted my nostrils.

It was a most peculiar room, the walls of which were covered over with some warm, white, soft, quilted stuff, studded all over with frosted silver buttons; the floor was covered with the curly white fleece of young lambs; in the middle of the apartment stood a capacious couch, on which was thrown the skin of a huge polar bear. Over this single piece of furniture, an old silver lamp—evidently from some Byzantine church or some Eastern synagogue—shed a pale glimmering light, sufficient, however, to light up the dazzling whiteness of this temple of Priapus whose votaries we were.

'I know,' said he, as he dragged me in, 'I know that white is your favorite color, that it suits your dark complexion, so it has been fitted up for you and you alone. No other mortal shall ever set foot in it.'

Uttering these words, he stripped me deftly of all my clothes—for I was in his hands like a slumbering child, or a man in a trance.

In an instant I was not only stark naked, but stretched on the bearskin, while he, standing in front of me, was gloating upon me with famished eyes.

I felt his glances greedily fall everywhere; they sank into my brain, and my head began to swim; they pierced through my heart, whipping my blood up, making it flow quicker and hotter through all the arteries; they darted within my veins, and Priapus unhooded itself and lifted up its head violently so that all the tangled web of veins in its body seemed ready to burst.

Then he felt me with his hands everywhere, after which he began to press his lips on every part of my body, showering kisses on my breast, my arms, my legs, my thighs, and then, when he had reached my middle parts, he pressed his face rapturously on the thick and curly hair that grows there so plentifully.

He shivered with delight as he felt the crisp locks upon his cheek and neck; then, taking hold of my phallus, he pressed his lips upon it. That seemed to electrify him; and then the tip and afterwards the whole glans disappeared within his mouth.

As it did so, I could hardly keep quiet. I clasped within my hands his curly and scented head; a shiver ran through my whole body; all my nerves were on edge; the sensation was so keen that it almost maddened me.

Then the whole column was in his mouth, the tip was touching his palate; his tongue, flattened or thickened, tickled me everywhere. Now I was sucked greedily, then nibbled or bitten. I screamed, I called on him to stop. I could not bear such intensity any longer; it was killing me. If it had lasted but a second longer I should have lost my senses. He was deaf and ruthless to my entreaties. Flashes of lightning seemed to be passing before my eyes; a torrent of fire was coursing through my body.

'Enough—stop, enough!' I groaned.

My nerves were extended; a thrill came over me; the soles of my feet seemed to have been drilled through. I writhed; I was convulsed.

One of his hands which had been caressing my testicles slipped under my bum—a finger was slipped in the hole. I seemed to be a man in front, a woman behind, for the pleasure I felt either way.

My trepidation had reached its climax. My brain reeled; my body melted; the burning milk of life was again mounting up, like a sap of fire; my bubbling blood mounted up to my brain, maddening me. I was exhausted; I fainted with pleasure: I fell upon him—a lifeless mass!

In a few minutes I was myself again—eager to take his place, and to return the caresses I had just received.

I tore the clothes from his body, so that he was speedily as naked as I was. What a pleasure it was to feel his skin against mine from head to foot! Moreover, the delight I had just felt had only increased my eagerness, so that, after clasping each other and wrestling together for a few moments, we both rolled on the floor, twisting, and rubbing, and crawling, and writhing, like two heated cats exciting each other into a paroxysm of rage.

But my lips were eager to taste his phallus—an organ which might have served as a model for the huge idol in the temple of Priapus, or over the doors of the Pompeian brothels, only that at the sight of this wingless god most men would have—as many did—discarded women for the love of their fellow men. It was big without having the proportion of an ass'; it was thick and rounded, though slightly tapering; the glans—a fruit of flesh and blood, like a small apricot—looked pulpy, round and appetizing.

I feasted my hungry eyes upon it; I handled it; I kissed it; I felt its soft glossy skin upon my lips; it moved with an inward motion of its own, as I did so. My tongue then deftly tickled the tip, trying to dart itself between those tiny rosy lips that, bulged out with love, opened and spattered a tiny drop of sparkling dew. I felt it quivering with a life of its own; I moved quicker, quicker, quicker. He clasped my head furiously; all his nerves were throbbing.

'Your mouth is burning—you are sucking

out my very brain! Stop, stop! my whole body is aglow! I can't—any more! I can't—it is too much!'

He grasped my head tightly to make me stop, but I pressed his phallus tightly with my lips, my cheeks, my tongue; my movements were more and more rapid, so that after a few strokes I felt him shudder from head to foot, as if seized by a fit of giddiness. He sighed, he groaned, he screamed. His head reeled; the pleasure he felt was so sharp that it verged upon pain.

'Stop, stop!' he moaned faintly, shutting his eyes and panting.

I, however, was maddened by the idea that he was now truly mine; that I was drinking down the fiery foaming sap of his body, the real elixir of life.

His arms for a moment clasped me convulsively. A rigidity then came over him; he was shattered by such an excess of wantonness.

I myself felt almost as much as he did, for in my fury I provoked an abundant ejaculation; and at the same time small drops of the same fluid which I was receiving in me, coursed slowly, painfully, out of my body. As this happened, our nerves relaxed and we fell exhausted upon one another.

A short space of rest—I cannot tell how long, intensity not being measured by Time's sedate pace—and then I felt his nerveless penis reawaken from its sleep, and press against my face; it was evidently trying to find my mouth, just like a greedy but glutted baby even in its sleep holds firm the nipple of its mother's breast simply for the pleasure of having it in its mouth.

I pressed my mouth upon it, and, like a young cock awakened at early dawn stretches forth its neck and crows lustily, it thrust its head towards my warm, pouted lips.

As soon as I had it in my mouth, Teleny wheeled himself around, and placed himself in the same position that I was to him, only with the difference that I was on my back and he was over me.

He began to kiss my rod; he played with the bushy hair that grew around it; he patted my buttocks, and, especially, he caressed my testicles with a knack all his own that filled me with unutterable delight.

His hands so increased the pleasure his mouth and his own phallus were giving me that I was soon beyond myself with excitement.

Our two bodies were one mass of quivering sensuality; and although we were both increasing the rapidity of our movements, still we were so maddened with lust that in that tension of the nerves the seminal glands refused to do their work.

We labored on in vain. My reason all at once left me; the parched blood within me vainly tried to ooze out, and it seemed to swirl in my injected eyes; it tingled in my ears. I was in a paroxysm of erotic rage—in a paroxysm of mad delirium.

My brain seemed trepanned, my spine sawn in two. All at once the gates of the sperm ducts were opened, and from hellish fires we were uplifted, amidst a shower of burning sparks, into a delightfully calm and ambrosial Olympus.

After a few moments' rest I uplifted myself on my elbow, and delighted my eyes with my lover's fascinating beauty. He was a very model of carnal comeliness; his chest was broad and strong, his arms rounded; in fact, I have never seen such a vigorous and at the same time agile frame; for not only was there not the slightest fat but not even the least superfluous flesh about him. He was all nerve, muscle, and sinew. It was his well-knit and supple joints that gave him the free, easy, and graceful motion so characteristic of the Felidae, of which he had also the flexibility, for when he clasped himself to you he seemed to entwine himself around you like a snake. Moreover, his skin was of a pearly almost iridescent whiteness, while the hair on the different parts of his body was quite black.

Teleny opened his eyes, stretched his arms towards me, took hold of my hand, kissed, and then bit me on the nape of my neck; then he showered a number of kisses all along my back, which, following one another in quick succession, seemed like a rain of rose-leaves falling from some full-blown flower.

Then he reached the two fleshy lobes which he pressed open with his hands, and darted his tongue in that hole where a little while before he had thrust his finger. This likewise was for me a new and thrilling sensation.

This done, he rose and stretched forth his hand to lift me up.

'Now,' said he, 'let us go in the next room, and see if we can find something to eat; for I think we really require some food, though, perhaps, a bath would not be amiss before we sit down to supper. Should you like to have one?'

'It might put you to inconvenience.'

For all answer he ushered me into a kind of cell, all filled with ferns and feathery palms, that—as he showed me—received during the day the rays of the sun from a skylight overhead.

'This is a kind of makeshift for a hothouse and a bathroom, which every habitable dwelling ought to have. I am too poor to have either, still this hole is big enough for my ablutions, and my plants seem to thrive pretty well in this warm and damp atmosphere.'

'But it's a princely bathroom!'

'No, no!' he said, smiling; 'it's an artist's bathroom.'

We at once plunged into the warm water, scented with essence of heliotrope; and it was so pleasant to rest there locked in each other's arms after our last excesses.

'I could stay here all night,' he mused; 'it is so delightful to handle you in this warm water. But you must be famished, so we had better go and get something to satisfy the inward cravings.'

We got out, and wrapped ourselves up for a moment with hot *peignoirs* of Turkish towelling.

'Come,' said he, 'let me lead you to the diningroom.'

I stood hesitating, looking first at my nakedness, then upon his. He smiled, and kissed me.

'You don't feel cold, do you?'

'No, but—'

'Well, then, don't be afraid; there is no one in the house. Everyone is asleep in the other flats, and besides, every window is tightly shut, and all the curtains are down.'

He dragged me with him into a neighboring room all covered with thick, soft, and silky carpets, the prevailing tone of which was dull Turkish red.

In the center of this apartment hung a curiously-wrought, star-shaped lamp, which the faithful—even nowadays—light on Friday eve.

We sat down on a soft-cushioned divan, in front of one of these ebony Arab tables all inlaid with colored ivory and iridescent mother-of-pearl.

'I cannot give you a banquet, although I expected you; still, there is enough to satisfy your hunger, I hope.'

There were some luscious Cancale oysters— few, but of an immense size; a dusty bottle of Sauterne, then a *paté de foie gras* highly scented with Perigord truffles; a partridge, with *paprika* or Hungarian curry, and a salad made out of a huge Piedmont truffle, as thinly sliced as shavings; and a bottle of exquisite dry sherry.

All these delicacies were served in dainty blue old Delft and Savona ware, for he had already heard of my hobby for old majolica.

Then came a dish of Seville oranges, bananas, and pineapples, flavored with Maraschino and covered with sifted sugar. It was a savory, tasty, tart and sweet medley, combining together the flavor and perfume of all these delicious fruits.

After having washed it down with a bottle of sparkling champagne, we then sipped some tiny cups of fragrant and scalding Mocha coffee; then he lighted a narghile, or Turkish water pipe, and we puffed at intervals the odorous Latakiah, inhaling it with our ever-hungry kisses from each other's mouths.

The fumes of the smoke and those of the wine rose up to our heads, and in our reawakened sensuality we soon had between our lips a far more fleshy mouthpiece than the amber one of the Turkish pipe.

Our heads were again soon lost between each other's thighs. We had once more but one body between us, juggling with one another, ever seeking new caresses, new sensations, a sharper and more inebriating kind of lewdness in our anxiety not only to enjoy ourselves but to make the other one feel. We were, therefore, very soon the prey of a blasting lust, and only some inarticulate sounds expressed the climax of our voluptuous state, until, more dead than alive, we fell upon each other—a mingled mass of shivering flesh.

After half an hour's rest and a bowl of arrak, curacoa and whisky punch, flavored with many hot, invigorating spices, our mouths were again pressed together.

His moist lips grazed mine so very slightly that I hardly felt their touch; they thus only awakened in me the eager desire to feel their contact more closely, while the tip of his tongue kept tantalizing mine, darting in my mouth for a second and rapidly slipping out again. His hands in the meanwhile passed over the most delicate parts of my body as lightly as a soft summer breeze passes over the smooth surface of the waters, and I felt my skin shiver with delight.

I happened to be lying on some cushions on the couch, which thus elevated me to Teleny's height; he swiftly put my legs on his shoulders, then, bending down his head, he began first to kiss, and then to dart his pointed tongue in my bum, thrilling me with an ineffable pleasure. Then rising when he had deftly prepared it well all around, he tried to press the tip of his phallus into it, but though he pressed hard, still he could not succeed in getting it in.

'Let me moisten it a little, and then it will slip in more easily.' I waited impatiently as he did so.

'Now,' said I, 'let us enjoy together that pleasure which the gods themselves did not disdain to teach us.'

He once more pressed the glans upon it; the tiny little lips protruded themselves within the gap; the tip worked its way inside, but the pulpy flesh bulged out all around, and the rod was thus arrested in its career.

'I am afraid I am hurting you?' he asked, 'had we not better leave it for some other time?'

'Oh, no! it is such a happiness to feel your body entering into mine.'

He thrust gently but firmly; the strong muscles of the anus relaxed; the glans was fairly lodged; the skin extended to such a degree that tiny, ruby beads of blood trickled from all around the splitting orifice; still, notwithstanding the way I was torn, the pleasure I felt was much greater than the pain.

He gave a sudden heave. The Rubicon was crossed; the column began to slide softly in; he could begin his pleasurable work.

I then saw his beautiful eyes gazing deep into mine. What unfathomable eyes they were! Like the sky or the main, they seemed to reflect the infinite. Never again shall I see eyes so full of burning love, of such smouldering languor. His glances had a mesmeric spell over me; they bereft me of my reason; they did even more—they changed sharp pain into delight.

I was in a state of ecstatic joy; all my nerves contracted and twitched. As he felt himself thus clasped and gripped, he shivered, he ground his teeth; he was unable to bear such a strong shock; his outstretched arms held fast my shoulders; he dug his nails into my flesh; he tried to move, but he was so tightly wedged and grasped that it was impossible to push himself any further in. Moreover, his strength was beginning to fail him, and he could then hardly stand upon his feet.

As he tried to give another jerk, I myself, that very moment, squeezed the whole rod with all the strength of my muscles, and a most violent jet, like a hot geyser, escaped from him, and coursed within me like some scorching, corroding poison; it seemed to set my blood on fire, and transmuted it into some kind of hot, intoxicating alcohol. His breath was thick and convulsive; his sobs choked him; he was utterly done in.

'I am dying!' he gasped out, his chest heaving with emotion; 'it is too much.' And he fell senseless in my arms.

After half an hour's rest he woke up, and began at once to kiss me with rapture, while his loving eyes beamed with thankfulness.

'You have made me feel what I never felt before.'

'Nor I either,' said I, smiling.

'I really did not know whether I was in heaven or in hell. I had quite lost my senses.'

He stopped for a moment to look at me, and then, 'How I love you, my Camille!' he went on, showering kisses on me; 'I have loved you to distraction from the very first moment I saw you.'

Then I began to tell him how I had suffered in trying to overcome my love for him; how I was haunted by his presence day and night; how happy I was at last.

'And now you must take my place. You must make me feel what you felt. You will be active and I passive; but we must try another position, for it is really tiresome to stand after all the fatigue we have undergone.'

'And what am I to do, for you know I am quite a novice?'

'Sit down there,' he replied, pointing to a stool constructed for the purpose, 'I'll ride on you while you impale me as if I were a woman. It is a mode of locomotion of which the ladies are so fond that they put it into practice whenever they get the slightest chance. My mother actually rode a gentleman under my very eyes. I was in the parlor when a friend happened to call, and had I been sent out suspicion might have been aroused, so I was made to believe that I was a very naughty little boy, and I was put in a corner with my face to the wall. Moreover, she told me that if I cried or turned round she'd put me to bed; but if I were good she'd give me a cake. I obeyed for one or two minutes, but after that, hearing an unusual rustle, and a loud breathing and panting, I saw what I could not understand at the time, but what was made clear to me many years afterwards.'

He sighed, shrugged his shoulders, then smiled and added—'Well, sit down there.'

I did as I was bidden. He first knelt down to say his prayers to Priapus, and having bathed and tickled the little god, he got astrad-

dle over me. As he had already lost his maidenhood long ago, my rod entered far more easily
in him than his had done in me, nor did I give
him the pain that I had felt, although my tool
is of no mean size.

He stretched himself open, the tip entered,
he moved a little, half the phallus was plunged
in; he pressed down, lifted himself up, then
came down again; after one or two strokes the
whole turgid column was lodged within his
body. When he was well impaled he put his
arms round my neck, and hugged and kissed me.

'Do you regret having given yourself to me?'
he asked, pressing me convulsively as if afraid
to lose me.

My penis, which seemed to wish to give its
own answer, wriggled within his body. I looked
deep into his eyes.

'Do you think it would have been more pleasant to be now lying in the slush of the river?'

He shuddered and kissed me, then eagerly,—
'How can you think of such horrible things just
now; it is real blasphemy to the Mysian god.'

Thereupon he began to ride a Priapean race
with masterly skill; from an amble he went on
to a trot, then to a gallop, lifting himself on
the tips of his toes, and coming down again
quicker and ever quicker.

A rigid tension of the nerves took place. My
heart was beating in such a way that I could
hardly breathe. All the arteries seemed ready
to burst. My skin was parched with a glowing

heat; a subtle fire coursed through my veins instead of blood.

Still he went on, quicker and quicker. I writhed in a delightful torture. I was melting away, but he never stopped till he had quite drained me of the last drop of life-giving fluid there was in me. My eyes were swimming in their socketes. I felt my heavy lids half close themselves; an unbearable voluptuousness of mingled pain and pleasure shattered my body and blasted my very soul; then everything waned in me. He clasped me in his arms, and I swooned away while he was kissing my cold and languid lips.

On the morrow the events of the night before seemed like a rapturous dream.

—Still, you must have felt rather seedy, after the many—

—Seedy? No, not at all. Nay, I felt the 'clear keen joyance' of the lark that loves, but 'ne'er knew love's sad satiety.' Hitherto, the pleasure that women had given me had always jarred upon my nerves. It was, in fact, 'a thing wherein we feel there is a hidden want.' Lust was now the overflowing of the heart and of the mind —the pleasurable harmony of all the senses.

The world that had hitherto seemed to me so bleak, so cold, so desolate, was now a perfect paradise; the air, although the barometer had fallen considerably, was crisp, light, and balmy; the sun—a round, furbished, copper disc, and more like a red Indian's backside than fair Apollo's effulgent face—was shining gloriously for me; the murky fog itself, that brought on dark night at three o'clock in the afternoon, was only a hazy mist that veiled all that was ungainly, and rendered Nature fantastic, and home so snug and cozy. Such is the power of the imagination.

You laugh! Alas! Don Quixote was not the only man who took windmills for giants, or barmaids for princesses. If your sluggish-brained, thick-pated costermonger never falls into such a trance as to mistake apples for potatoes; if your grocer never turns hell into heaven, or heaven into hell—well, they are sane people who weigh everything in the well-poised scale of reason. Try and shut them up in nutshells, and you will see if they would deem themselves monarchs of the world. They, unlike Hamlet, always see things as they really are. I never did. But then, you know, my father died mad.

Anyhow, that overpowering weariness, that loathsomeness of life, had now quite passed away. I was blithe, merry, happy. Teleny was my lover; I was his.

Far from being ashamed of my crime, I felt that I should like to proclaim it to the world. For the first time in my life I understood that lovers could be so foolish as to entwine their initials together. I felt like carving his name on the bark of trees, that the birds seeing it might twitter it from morn till eventide; that the breeze might lisp it to the rustling leaves of the forest. I wished to write it on the shingle of the beach, that the ocean itself might know of my love for him, and murmur it everlastingly.

—Still I had thought that on the morrow—the intoxication passed—you would have shuddered at the thought of having a man for a lover?

—Why? Had I committed a crime against nature when my own nature found peace and happiness thereby? If I was thus, surely it was the fault of my blood, not myself. Who had planted nettles in my garden? Not I. They had grown there unawares, from my very childhood. I began to feel their carnal stings long before I could understand what conclusion they imported. When I had tried to bridle my lust, was it my fault if the scale of reason was far too light to balance that of sensuality? Was I to blame if I could not argue down my raging motion? Fate, Iago-like, had clearly showed me that if I would damn myself, I could do so in a more delicate way than drowning. I yielded to my destiny, and encompassed my joy.

Withal, I never said with Iago,—'Virtue, a fig!' No, virtue is the sweet flavor of the peach; vice, the tiny droplet of prussic acid—its delicious savor. Life, without either, would be vapid.

—Still, not having, like most of us, been inured to sodomy from your schooldays, I should have thought that you would have been loath to have yielded your body to another man's pleasure.

—Loath? Ask the virgin if she regrets having given up her maidenhood to the lover she dotes on, and who fully returns her love? She has lost a treasure that all the wealth of Golconda cannot buy again; she is no longer what the world calls a pure, spotless, immaculate lily, and not having had the serpent's guile in her, society—the lilies—will brand her with an infamous name; profligates will leer at her, the pure will turn away in scorn. Still, does the girl regret having yielded her body for love— the only thing worth living for? No. Well, no more did I. Let 'clay-cold heads and lukewarm hearts' scourge me with their wrath if they will.

On the morrow, when we met again, all traces of fatigue had passed away. We rushed into each other's arms and smothered ourselves with kisses, for nothing is more an incentive to love than a short separation. What is it that renders married ties unbearable? The too-great intimacy, the sordid cares, the triviality of everyday life. The young bride must love indeed if she feels no disappoinmtent when she sees her mate just awakened from a fit of tough snoring, seedy, unshaven, with braces and slippers, and hears him clear his throat and spit— for men actually spit, even if they do not indulge in other rumbling noises.

The husband, likewise, must love indeed, not to feel an inward sinking when a few days after the wedding he finds his bride's middle parts tightly tied up in foul and bloody rags. Why did not nature create us like birds—or rather, like midges—to live but one summer day—a long day of love?

On the night of this next day Teleny surpassed himself at the piano; and when the ladies had finished waving their tiny handkerchiefs, and throwing flowers at him, he stole away from a host of congratulating admirers, and came to meet me in my carriage, waiting for him at the door of the theatre; then we drove away to his house. I passed that night with him, a night not of unbroken slumbers, but of inebriating bliss.

As true votaries of the Grecian god, we poured out seven copious libations to Priapus—for seven is a mystic, cabalistic, propitious number—and in the morning we tore ourselves from each other's arms, vowing everlasting love and fidelity; but, alas! what is there immutable in the ever-changing world, except, perhaps, the sleep eternal in the eternal light.

—And your mother?

—She perceived that a great change had been wrought in me. Now, far from being crabbed and waspish, like an old maid that cannot find rest anywhere, I was even-tempered and good-humored. She, however, attributed the change to the tonics I was taking, little guessing the real nature of these tonics. Later, she thought

I must have some kind of *liaison* or other, but did not interfere with my private affairs; she knew that the time for sowing my wild oats had come, and she left me complete freedom of action.

—Well, you were a lucky fellow.

—Yes, but perfect happiness cannot last long. Hell gapes on the threshold of heaven, and one step plunges us from ethereal light into Cerebian darkness. So it has ever been with me in this checkered life of mine. A fortnight after that memorable night of unbearable anguish and of thrilling delight, I awoke in the midst of felicity to find myself in thorough wretchedness.

One morning, as I went in to breakfast, I found on the table a note which the postman had brought the evening before. I never received letters at home, having hardly any correspondence, save a business one, which was always transacted at the office. The handwriting was unknown to me. It must be some tradesman, thought I, leisurely buttering my bread. At last I tore the envelope open. It was a card of two lines without any address or signature.

—And—?

—Have you ever by accident placed your hand on a strong galvanic battery, and got through your fingers a shock that for a moment bereaves you of your very reason? If so, you can have but a faint impression of what that bit of paper produced on my nerves. I was stunned by it. Having read those few words I saw nothing more, for the room began to spin round me.

—Well, but what was there to terrify you in such a way?

—Only these few harsh, grating words that have remained indelibly engraved on my mind.

'If you do not give up your lover T. . . you shall be branded as an *enculé.*'

This horrible, infamous, anonymous threat, in all its crude harshness, came so unexpectedly that it was, as the Italians express it, like a clap of thunder on a bright sunshiny day.

Little dreaming of its contents, I had opened it carelessly in my mother's presence; but hardly had I perused it than a state of utter prostration came over me, so that I had not even strength enough to hold up that tiny bit of paper.

My hands were trembling like aspen leaves—nay, my whole body was quivering; so thoroughly was I cowed down with fear and appalled with shame.

All the blood fled from my cheeks, my lips were cold and clammy; an icy perspiration was on my brow; I felt myself growing pale, and I knew that my cheeks must have been of an ashen, livid hue.

Nevertheless, I tried to master my emotion. I lifted up a spoonful of coffee to my mouth; but, ere it had reached my lips, I gagged, and was ready to throw up. The pitching and tossing of a boat on the heaviest sea could not have brought about such a state of sinking sickness as that with which my body was then convulsed. Nor could Macbeth, upon seeing Banquo's murdered ghost, have been more terrified than I was.

What was I to do? To be proclaimed a sodomite in the face of the world, or to give up the man who was dearer to me than life itself? No, death was preferable to either.

—And still, you said just now that you would have liked the whole world to know your love for the pianist.

—I admit that I did, and I do not deny it; but have you ever understood the contradictions of the human heart?

—Moreover, you did not consider sodomy a crime?

—No; had I done society any harm by it?

—Then why were you so terrified?

—Once a lady on her reception day asked her little boy—a lisping child of three—where his papa was?

'In his room,' said he.

'What is he doing?' asked the imprudent mother.

'He is making proots,' replied the urchin, innocently, in a high treble, loud enough to be heard by everyone in the room.

Can you imagine the feelings of the mother, or those of the wife, when, a few moments afterwards, her husband came into the room? Well, the poor man told me that he almost regarded himself as a branded man, when his blushing wife told him of his child's indiscretion. Still, had he committed a crime?

Who is the man that, at least once in his lifetime, has not felt a perfect satisfaction in breaking wind, or, as the child onomatopoetically expressed it, making a 'proot'? What was there, then, to be ashamed of; that surely was no crime against nature?

The fact is, that nowadays we have got to be so mealy-mouthed, so over-nice, that Madame Eglantine, who 'raught full semely after her meat' would be looked upon, in spite of her stately manners, as something worse than a scullery-maid. We have become so demurely prim that every member of Parliament will soon have to provide himself with a certificate of morality from the clergyman, or the Sabbath-school teacher, before he is allowed to take possession of his seat. At any cost, appearances must be saved; for ranting editors are jealous gods, and their wrath is implacable, for it pays well, as good people like to know what naughty folks do.

—And who was the person who had written those lines to you?

—Who? I cudgelled my brain, and it evoked a number of specters, all of which were as impalpable and as frightful as Milton's death; all threatened to hurl at me a deadly dart. I even fancied for an instant, that it was Teleny, just to see the extent of my love for him.

—It was the Countess, was it not?

—I thought so, too. Teleny was not a man to be loved by halves, and a woman madly in love is capable of everything. Still, it seemed hardly probable that a lady would use such a weapon; and moreover, she was away. No, it was not, it could not be, the Countess. But who was it? Everybody and nobody.

For a few days I was tortured so incessantly that at times I felt as if I were growing mad. My nervousness increased to such a pitch that I was actually afraid to leave the house for fear of meeting the writer of that loathsome note.

Like Cain, it seemed as if I carried my crime written upon my brow. I saw a sneer upon the face of every man that looked at me. A finger was forever pointing at me; a voice, loud enough for all to hear, was whispering, 'The sodomite!'

Going to my office, I heard a man walking behind me. I went on quickly; he hastened his step. I almost began to run. All at once a hand was laid on my shoulder. I was about to faint with terror. At that moment I almost expected to hear the awful words,—'In the name of the law I arrest you, sodomite!'

The creaking of a door made me shiver; the sight of a letter appalled me.

Was I conscience-striken? No, it was simply fear—abject fear, not remorse. Moreover, is not a sodomite liable to be condemned to perpetual imprisonment?

You must think me a coward, but after all even the bravest man can only face an open foe. The thought that the occult hand of an unknown enemy is always uplifted against you, and ready to deal you a mortal blow, is unbearable. Today you are a man of a spotless reputation; tomorrow, a single word uttered against you in the street by a hired ruffian, a paragraph in a ranting paper by one of the modern *bravi* of the press, and your fair name is blasted forevermore.

—And your mother?

—Her attention had been drawn elsewhere when I opened my letter. She only remarked my paleness a few moments afterwards. I therefore told her that I was not feeling well, and seeing me retching she believed me; in fact, she was afraid I had caught some illness.

—And Teleny—what did he say?

—I did not go to him that day, I only sent him word that I would see him on the morrow.

What a night I passed! First I kept up as long as I could, for I dreaded going to bed. At last, weary and worn out, I undressed and lay down; but my bed seemed electrified, for all my nerves began to twitch, and a feeling of creepiness came over me.

I felt distracted. I tossed about for some time; then, frightened lest I should grow mad, I got up, went stealthily to the dining room and got a bottle of cognac, and returned to my bedchamber. I drank down about half a tumbler, and then went again to bed.

Unaccustomed to such strong drink I went off to sleep; but was it sleep?

I awoke in the middle of the night, dreaming

that Catherine, our maid, had accused me of having murdered her, and that I was about to be tried.

I got up, poured myself another glass of spirits, and again found oblivion if not rest.

On the morrow I again sent word to Teleny that I could not see him, although I longed to do so; but the day after that, seeing that I did not come to him as usual, he called upon me.

Surprised at the physical and moral change which had come over me, he began to think that some mutual friend had been slandering him, so to reassure him, I—after much pressing and many questions—took out that loathsome letter which I as much dreaded to touch as if it had been a viper, and gave it to him.

Although more than myself inured to such matters, his brow grew cloudy and thoughtful, and he even went pale. Still, after pondering over it for a moment, he began to examine the paper on which those horrible words were written; then he lifted up both card and envelope to his nose, and smelt them both. A merry expression came all at once over his face. 'I have it—I have it—you need not be afraid! They smell of attar of roses,' cried he; 'I know who it is.'

'Who?'

'Why! can't you guess?'

'The Countess?'

Teleny frowned.

'How is it you know about her?'

I told him all. When I had finished, he clasped me in his arms and kissed me again and again.

'I tried in every way to forget you, Camille, you see if I succeeded. The Countess is now miles away and we shall not see each other again.'

As he said these words my eyes fell on a very fine yellow diamond ring—a moonstone—which he wore on his little finger.

'That is a woman's ring,' I said, 'she gave it to you?'

He made no answer.

'Will you wear this one in its stead?'

The ring I gave him was an antique cameo of exquisite workmanship, surrounded with brilliants, but its chief merit was that it represented the head of Antinous.

'But,' said he, 'this is a priceless jewel'; and he looked at it closer. Then taking my head between his hands, and covering my face with kisses,—'Priceless indeed to me, for it looks like you.'

I burst out laughing.

'Why do you laugh?' said he, astonished.

'Beacuse,' was my reply, 'the features are quite yours.'

'Perhaps, then,' he said, 'we are alike in looks as well as in tastes. Who knows—you are, perhaps, my *doppelganger*? Then, woe to one of us!'

'Why?'

'In our country they say that a man must never meet his *alter ego*, it brings misfortune to one or to both'; and he shivered as he said this. Then, with a smile, 'I am superstitious, you know.'

'Anyhow,' I added, 'should any misfortune part us, let this ring, like that of the virgin queen, be your messenger. Send it to me and I swear that nothing shall keep me away from you.'

The ring was on his finger and he was in my arms. Our pledge was sealed with a kiss.

He then began to whisper words of love in a low, sweet, hushed, and cadenced tone that seemed like a distant echo of sounds heard in a half-remembered ecstatic dream. They mounted up to my brain like the bubbles of some effervescent, intoxicating love-philter. I can even now hear them ringing in my ear. Nay, as I remember them again, I feel a shiver of sensuality creep all over my body, and that insatiable desire he always excited in me kindles my blood.

He was sitting by my side, as close to me as I am now to you; his shoulder was leaning on my shoulder, exactly as yours is.

First he passed his hand on mine, but so gently that I could hardly feel it; then slowly his fingers began to lock themselves within mine, just like this; for he seemed to delight in taking possession of me inch by inch.

After that, one of his arms encircled my waist, then he put the other round my neck, and the tips of his fingers twiddled and fondled my throat, thrilling me with delight.

As he did so, our cheeks slightly grazed each other; and that touch—perhaps because it was so imperceptible—vibrated through all my body, giving all the nerves around the veins a not unpleasant twinge. Our mouths were now in close contact, and still he did not kiss me; his lips were simply tantalizing mine, as if to make me more keenly conscious of our nature's affinity.

The nervous state in which I had been these last days rendered me ever so much the more excitable. I therefore longed to feel that pleasure which cools the blood and calms the brain, but he seemed disposed to prolong my eagerness, and to make me reach that pitch of inebriating sensuality that verges upon madness.

At last, when neither of us could bear our excitement any longer, we tore off our clothes, and then naked we rolled, the one on the other, like two snakes, trying to feel as much of each other as we could. To me it seemed that all the pores of my skin were tiny mouths that pouted out to kiss him.

'Clasp me—grip me—hug me!—tighter—tighter still! that I may enjoy your body!'

My rod, as tough as a piece of iron, slipped between his legs; and feeling itself tweaked, began to water, and a few tiny, viscid drops oozed out.

Seeing the way in which I was tortured, he at last took pity upon me. He bent down his head upon my phallus, and began to kiss it.

I, however, did not wish to taste this delightful pleasure by halves, or to enjoy this thrilling rapture alone. We therefore shifted our position, and in a twinkling I had in my mouth the thing at which he was tweaking so delightfully.

Soon that acrid milk, like the sap of the fig tree or the euphorbia, which seems to flow from the brain and the marrow, spouted out, and in its stead a jet of caustic fire was coursing through every vein and artery, and all my nerves were vibrating as if set in motion by some strong electric current.

Finally, the paroxysm of pleasure which is the delirium of sensuality began to abate, and I was left crushed and annihilated; then a pleasant state of torpor followed, and my eyes closed for a few seconds in happy oblivion.

Having recovered my senses, my eyes again fell on the repulsive, anonymous note; and I shuddered and nestled myself against Teleny as if for protection, so loathsome was truth, even then, to me.

'But you have not told me yet who wrote those horrible words.'

'Who? Why, the general's son, of course.'

'What! Briancourt?'

'Who else can it be. No one except him can have an inkling of our love; Briancourt, I am sure, has been watching us. Besides, look here,' he added, picking up the bit of paper, 'not wanting to write on paper with his crest or initials, and probably not having any other, he has written on a cartel deftly cut out of a piece of drawing paper. Who else but a painter could have done such a thing? By taking too many precautions, we sometimes compromise ourselves.

Moreover, smell it. He is so saturated with attar of roses that everything he touches is impregnated with it.'

'Yes, you are right,' said I, musingly.

'Over and above all this, it is just the thing for him to do, not that he is bad at heart—'

'You love him!' said I, with a pang of jealousy, grasping his arm.

'No, I do not; but I am simply just towards him; besides you have known him from his childhood, and you must admit that he is not so bad, is he?'

'No, he is simply mad.'

'Mad? Well, perhaps a little more so than other men,' said my friend, smiling.

'What! you think all men crazy?'

'I only know one sane man—my shoemaker. He is only mad once a week—on Monday, when he gets jolly drunk.'

'Well, don't let us talk of madness any more. My father died mad, and I suppose that, sooner or later—'

'You must know,' said Teleny, interrupting me, 'that Briancourt has been in love with you for a long time.'

'With me?'

'Yes, but he thinks you dislike him.'

'I never was remarkably fond of him.'

'Now that I think it over, I believe that he would like to have us both together, so that we might form a kind of trinity of love and bliss.'

'And you think he tried to bring it about in that way.'

'In love and in war, every stratagem is good; and perhaps with him as with the Jesuits, "the end justifies the means," Anyhow, forget this note completely, let it be like a midwinter night's dream.'

Then, taking the obnoxious bit of paper, he placed it on the glowing embers; first it writhed and crackled, then a sudden flame burst forth and consumed it. An instant afterwards, it was nothing but a little, black, crumpled thing, on which tiny, fiery snakes were hastily chasing and then swallowing each other as they met.

Then came a puff from the crackling logs, and it mounted and disappeared up the chimney like a little black devil.

Naked as we were on the low couch in front of the fireplace, we clasped and hugged each other fondly.

'It seemed to threaten us before it disappeared, did it not? I hope Briancourt will never come between us.'

'We'll defy him,' said my friend, smiling; and taking hold of my phallus and of his own, he brandled them both. 'This,' said he, 'is the most efficent exorcism in Italy against the evil eye. Moreover he has doubtless forgotten both you and me by this time—nay, even the very idea of having written this note.'

'Why?'

'Because he has found a new lover.'

'Who, the Spahi officer?'

'No, a young Arab. Anyhow, we'll know who it is by the subject of the picture he is going to paint. Some time ago he was only dreaming of a pendant to the three Graces, which to him represented the mystic trinity of tribadism.'

A few days afterwards we met Briancourt in the green room of the Opera. When he saw us, he looked away and tried to shun us. I would have done the same.

'No,' said Teleny, 'let us go and speak to him and have matters out. In such things never show the slightest fear. If you face the enemy boldly, you have already half vanquished him.' Then, going up to him and dragging me with him,—'Well,' said he, stretching out his hand, 'what has become of you? It is some days since we have seen each other.'

'Of course,' he replied, 'new friends make us forget old ones.'

'Like new pictures old ones. By the bye, what sketch have you begun?'

'Oh, something glorious!—a picture that will make a mark, if any does.'

'But what is it?'

'Jesus Christ.'

'Jesus Christ?'

'Yes, since I knew Achmet, I have been able to understand the Saviour. You would love Him, too,' he added, 'if you could see those dark, mesmeric eyes, with their long and jetty fringe.'

'Love whom,' said Teleny, 'Achmet or Christ?'

'Christ, of course!' quoth Briancourt, shrugging his shoulders. 'You would be able to fathom the influence He must have had over the crowd. My Syrian need not speak to you, he lifts his eyes upon you and you grasp the meaning of his thoughts. Christ, likewise, never wasted His breath spouting cant to the multitude. He wrote on the sand and could thereby "look the world to law." As I was saying, I shall paint Achmet as the Saviour, and you,' he added to Teleny, 'as John, the disciple He loved; for the Bible clearly says and continually repeats that He loved this favorite disciple.'

'And how will you paint Him?'

'Christ erect, clasping John, who hugs Him, and who leans his head on his friend's bosom. Of course there must be something lovably soft and womanly in the disciple's look and attitude; he must have your visionary violet eyes and your voluptuous mouth. Crouched at their feet there will be one of the many adulterous Marys, but Christ and the other—as John modestly terms himself, as if he were his Master's mistress—look down at her with a dreamy, half-scornful, half-pitiful expression.'

'And will the people understand your meaning?'

'Anybody who has any sense will. Besides, to render my idea clearer, I'll paint a pendant to it: "Socrates—the Greek Christ, with Alcibiades, his favorite disciple." The woman will be Xantippe.' Then turning to me, he added, 'But you must promise to come and sit for Alcibiades.'

'Yes,' said Teleny, 'but on one condition.'

'Name it.'

'Why did you write Camille that note?'

'What note?' he asked, his face turning red.

'Come—no gammon!'

'How did you know I wrote it?'

'Like Zadig, I saw the traces of the dog's ears.'

'Well, as you know it's me, I'll tell you frankly, it was because I was jealous.'

'Of whom?'

'Of you both. Yes, you may smile, but it's true.'

Then turning towards me, 'I've known you since we both were but little more than toddling babies, and I've never had that from you,'—and he cracked his thumbnail on his upper teeth—'while he,' pointing to Teleny, 'comes, sees, and conquers. Anyhow, it'll be for some future time. Meanwhile, I bear you no grudge; nor do you for that stupid threat of mine, I'm sure.'

'You don't know what miserable days and sleepless nights you made me pass.'

'Did I? I'm sorry; forgive me. You know I'm mad—everyone says so,' he exclaimed, grasping both our hands; 'and now that we are friends you must come to my next symposium.'

'When is it to be?' asked Teleny.

'On Tuesday week.'

Then turning to me, 'I'll introduce you to a lot of pleasant fellows who'll be delighted to make your acquaintance, and many of whom have long been astonished that you are not one of us.'

The week passed quickly. Joy soon made me

forget the dreadful anxiety caused by Brian-court's card.

A few days before the night fixed for the feast,—'How shall we dress for the symposium?' asked Teleny.

'How? Is it to be a masquerade?'

'We all have our little hobbies. Some men like soldiers, others sailors; some are fond of tightrope dancers, others of dandies. There are men who, though in love with their own sex, only care for them in women's clothes. *L'habit ne fait pas le moine* is not always a truthful proverb, for you see that even in birds the males display their gayest plumage to captivate their mates.'

'And what clothes should you like me to wear, for you are the only being I care to please?' I said.

'None.'

'Oh! but—'

'You'll feel shy, to be seen naked?'

'Of course.'

'Well, then, a tight-fitting cycling suit; it shows off the figure best.'

'Very well; and you?'

'I'll always dress exactly as you do.'

On the evening in question we drove to the painter's studio, the outside of which was, if not quite dark, at least very dimly lighted. Teleny tapped three times, and after a little while Briancourt himself came to open.

Whatever faults the general's son had, his manners were those of the French nobility, therefore perfect; his stately gait might even have graced the court of the *grand Monarque;* his politeness was unrivalled—in fact, he possessed all those 'small, sweet courtesies of life,' which, as Sterne says, 'beget inclinations to love at first sight.' He was about to usher us in, when Teleny stopped him.

'Wait a moment,' said he, 'could not Camille have a peep at your harem first? You know he is but a neophyte in the Priapean creed. I am his first lover.'

'Yes, I know,' interrupted Briancourt, sighing, 'and I cannot say sincerely, may you long be the last.'

'And not being inured to the sight of such revelry he will be induced to run away like Joseph from Mrs. Potiphar.'

'Very well, do you mind giving yourself the trouble to come this way?'

And with these words he led us through a dimly-lighted passage and up a winding staircase into a kind of balcony made out of old Arab *moucharabie,* brought to him by his father from Tunis or Algiers.

'From here you can see everything without being seen, so ta-ta for a while, but not for long, as supper will soon be served.'

As I stepped in this kind of loggia and looked down into the room, I was, for a moment, if not dazzled, at least perfectly bewildered. It seemed as if from this everyday world of ours I had been transported into the magic realms of fairyland. A thousand lamps of varied form filled the room with a strong yet hazy light. There were wax tapers upheld by Japanese cranes, or glowing in massive bronze or silver candlesticks, the plunder of Spanish altars; star-shaped or octagonal lamps from Moorish mosques or Eastern synagogues; curiously-wrought iron cressets of tortured and fantastic designs; chandeliers of numerous, iridescent glasswork reflected in Dutch gilt, or Castel-Durante majolica sconces.

Though the room was very large, the walls were all covered with pictures of the most lascivious nature; for the general's son, who was very rich, painted mostly for his own delight. Many were only half-finished sketches, for his ardent yet fickle imagination could not dwell long on the same subject, nor could his talent for invention be long satisfied with the same way of painting.

In some of his imitations of the libidinous Pompeian encaustics he had tried to fathom the secrets of a bygone art. Some pictures were executed with the minute care and the corrosive paints of Leonardo da Vinci; while others looked more like Greuze's pastels, or wrought in Watteau's delicate hues. Some flesh tints had the golden haze of the Venetian school, while—

—Please finish this digression on Briancourt's paintings, and tell me something of the more realistic scene.

—Well, on faded old damask couches, on huge pillows made out of priests' stoles, worked by devout fingers in silver and in gold, on soft Persian and Syrian divans, on lion and panther rugs, on mattresses covered over with electric cats' skins, men, young and good-looking, almost all naked, were lounging there by twos and threes, grouped in attitudes of the most consummate lewdness such as the imagination can never picture to itself, and such as are only seen in the brothels of men in lecherous Spain, or in those of the wanton East.

—It must indeed have been a rare sight, seen from the cage in which you were cooped; and I suppose your cocks were crowing so lustily that the naked fellows below must have been in great danger of receiving a shower of your holy water, for you must have brandled each other's sprinklers rapturously up there.

—The frame was well worth the picture, for, as I was saying before, the studio was a museum of lewd art worthy of Sodom or of Babylon. Paintings, statues, bronzes, plaster casts— either masterpieces of Paphian art or of Priapean designs, emerged from amidst deep-tinted silks of velvety softness, amidst sparkling crystals, gem-like enamel, golden china or opaline majolica, varied with yataghans and Turkish sabers, with hilts and scabbards of gold and silver filigree mark, all studded with coral and turquoise, or other more sparkling precious stones.

From huge Chinese bowls rose costly ferns, dainty Indian palms, creeping plants and parasites, with wicked-looking flowers from American forests, and feathery grasses from the Nile in Sevres vases; while from above, ever and anon, a shower of full-blown red and pink roses came pouring down, mingling their intoxicating scent with that of the attar which ascended in white cloudlets from censers and silver chafing-dishes.

The perfume of that over-heated atmosphere, the sound of smothered sighs, the groans of pleasure, the smack of eager kisses expressing the never-satiated lust of youth, made my brain reel, while my blood was parched by the sight of those ever-changing lascivious attitudes, expressing the most maddening paroxysm of debauchery, which tried to soothe itself or to invent a more thrilling and intense sensuality, or sickening and fainting away under their excess of feeling, while milky sperm and ruby drops of blood dappled their naked thighs.

—It must have been a rapturous sight.

—Yes, but just then it seemed to me as if I were in some rank jungle, where everything that is beautiful brings about instant death; where gorgeous, venomous snakes cluster together and look like bunches of variegated flowers, where sweet blossoms are ever dropping wells of fiery poison.

Here, likewise, everything pleased the eye and galled the blood; here the silvery streaks on the dark-green satin, and there the argentine tracery on the smooth, prasinous leaves of the water-lilies, were only the slimy trail—here of man's creative power, there of some loathsome reptile.

'But look there,' I said to Teleny; 'there are also women.'

'No,' he replied, 'women are never admitted to our revels.'

'But look at that couple there. See that naked man with his hand under the skirts of the girl clasped against him.'

'Both are men.'

'What! also that one with the reddish-auburn hair and brilliant complexion? Why, is it not Viscount de Pontgrimaud's mistress?'

'Yes, the Venus d'Ille, as she is generally called; and the Viscount is down in a corner, but the Venus d'Ille is a man!'

I stared, astonished. What I had taken for a woman looked, indeed, like a beautiful bronze figure, as smooth and polished as a Japanese cast *à cire perdue,* with an enamelled Parisian cocotte's head.

Whatever the sex of this strange being was, he or she had on a tight-fitting dress of a changing color—gold in the light, dark green in the shade—silk gloves and stockings of the same tint as the satin of the dress, fitting so tightly on the rounded arms and most beautifully-shaped legs that these limbs looked as even and as hard as those of a bronze statue.

'And that other one there, with black ringlets, *accrochecoeurs,* in a dark blue velvet tea-gown, with bare arms and shoulders, is that lovely woman a man, too?'

'Yes, he is an Italian and a Marquis, as you can see by the crest on his fan. He belongs, moreover, to one of the oldest families of Rome. But look there. Briancourt has been repeatedly making signs to us to go down. Let us go.'

'No, no!' said I, clinging to Teleny; 'let us rather go away.'

Still, that sight had so heated my blood that, like Lot's wife, I stood there, gloating upon it.

'I'll do whatever you like, but I think that if we go away now you'll be sorry for it afterwards. Besides, what do you fear? Am I not with you? No one can part us. We shall remain all the evening together, for here it is not the same as in the usual balls, where men bring their wives in order that they may be clasped and hugged by the first comer who likes to waltz with them. Moreover, the sight of all those excesses will only give a zest to our own pleasure.'

'Well, let us go,' said I, rising; 'but stop. That man in a pearly-grey Eastern robe must be the Syrian; he has lovely almond-shaped eyes.'

'Yes, that is Achmet effendi.'

'Whom is he talking with? Is it not Briancourt's father?'

'Yes, the general is sometimes a passive guest at his son's little parties. Come, shall we go?'

'One moment more. Do tell me who is that man with eyes on fire? He seems, indeed, lust incarnate, and is evidently past-master in lewdness. His face is familiar, and still I cannot remember where I have seen him.'

'He is a young man who, having spent his fortune in the most unbridled debauchery without any damage to his constitution, has enlisted in the Spahis to see what new pleasures Algiers could afford him. That man is indeed a volcano. But here is Briancourt.'

'Well,' said he, 'are you going to stay up here in the dark all the evening?'

'Camille is abashed,' said Teleny, smiling.

'Then come in masked,' said the painter, dragging us down, and giving us each a black velvet half-mask before ushering us in.

The announcement that supper was waiting in the next room had almost brought the revel to a standstill.

As we entered the studio, the sight of our dark suits and masks seemed to throw a dampness on everyone. We were, however, soon surrounded by a number of young men who came to welcome and to fondle us, some of whom were old acquaintances.

After a few questions Teleny was known, and his mask was at once snatched off; but no one for a long time could make out who I was. I, in the meanwhile, kept ogling the middle parts of the naked men around me, the thick and curly hair of which sometimes covered the stomach and the thighs. Nay, that unusual sight excited me in such a way that I could hardly forbear handling those tempting organs; and had it not been for the love I bore Teleny, I should have done something more than finger them.

One phallus, especially—that of the Viscount

—caused my intense admiration. It was of such a size that had a Roman lady possessed it she would never have asked for an ass. In fact, every whore was frightened at it; and it was said that once, abroad, a woman had been ripped up by it, for he had thrust his tremendous instrument up into her womb, and slit the partition between the front and the back hole, so that the poor wretch had died in consequence of the wound received.

His lover, however, throve upon it, for he was not only artificially but also naturally of a most florid complexion. As this young man saw that I seemed to doubt what sex he belonged to, he pulled up the skirts he wore and showed me a dainty, pink-and-white penis, all surrounded by a mass of dark golden hair.

Just when everybody was begging me to take off my mask, and I was about to comply, Dr. Charles—usually called Charlemagne—who had been rubbing himself against me like an overheated cat, all at once clasped me in his arms and kissed me lustily.

'Well, Briancourt,' said he, 'I congratulate you upon your new acquisition. Nobody's presence could have given me more pleasure than Des Grieux's.'

Hardly had these words been uttered than a nimble hand snatched off my mask.

Ten mouths at least were ready to kiss me, a score of hands were fondling me; but Briancourt put himself between them and me.

'For this evening,' said he, 'Camille is like

a sugar-plum on a cake, something to be looked at and not touched. René and he are on their honeymoon yet, and this *fete* is given in their honor, and in that of my new lover Achmet effendi.' And, turning round, he introduced us to the young man whom he was to portray as Jesus Christ. 'And now,' said he, 'let us go in to supper.'

The room, or hall, into which we were led was furnished something like a triclinium, with beds or couches instead of chairs.

'My friend,' said the general's son, 'the supper is a scanty one, the courses are neither many nor abundant, the meal is rather to invigorate than to satiate. I hope, however, that the generous wines and stimulating drinks will enable us all to return to our pleasures with renewed eagerness.'

—Still, I suppose it was a supper worthy of Lucullus?

—I hardly remember it now. I only recollect that it was the first time I tasted *bouillabaisse*, and some sweet spiced rice made after the Indian recipe, and that I found both delicious.

I had Teleny on my couch beside me, and Dr. Charles was my next neighbor. He was a fine, tall, well-built, broad-shouldered man, with a fair-flowing beard, for which—as well as for his name and size—he had been nicknamed Chalemagne. I was surprised to see him wearing round his neck a fine Venetian gold chain, to which was hanging—as I first thought —a locket, but which, on closer examination, proved to be a gold laurel wreath studded with brilliants. I asked him if it were a talisman or a relic?

He, thereupon, standing up, — 'My friends, Des Grieux here—whose lover I fain would be —asks me what this jewel is; and as most of you have already put me the same question, I'll satisfy you all now, and hold my peace forevermore about it.

'This laurel wreath,' he said, holding it up between his fingers, 'is the reward of merit— or rather, I should say, of chastity: it is my *couronne de rosiere.* Having finished my medical studies and walked the hospitals, I found myself a doctor; but what I could never find was a single patient who would give me not twenty, but a single franc piece for all the physic I administered him. When, one day, Dr. N—n seeing my brawny arms—and in fact he had arms like a Hercules—recommended me to an old lady, whose name I'll not mention, for massage. In fact I went to this old dame, whose name is not Potiphar, and who, as I took off my coat and tucked up my sleeves, cast a longing glance upon my muscles and then seemed lost in meditation; afterwards I concluded that she was calculating the rule of proportions.

'Dr. N—n had told me that the weakness of the nerves in her lower limbs was from the knees downwards. She, however, seemed to think that it was from the knees upwards. I was ingenuously puzzled, and—not to make a mistake—I rubbed from the foot upwards; but soon I remarked that the higher I went the more softly she purred.

'After about ten minutes,—"I am afraid I am tiring you," said I; "perhaps it is enough for the first time."

' "Oh," replied she, with the languishing eyes of an old fish, "I could be rubbed by you the whole day. I already feel such a benefit. You have a man's hand for strength, a woman's for softness. But you must be tired, poor fellow! Now, what will you take — Madeira, or dry sherry?"

' "Nothing, thank you."

' "A glass of champagne and a biscuit?"

' "No, thanks."

' "You must take something. Oh, I know!—a tiny glass of Alkermes from the Certosa of Florence. Yes, I think I'll sip one with you myself. I already feel so much better for the rubbing." And thereupon she pressed my hand tenderly. "Will you have the kindness to ring?"

'I did so. We both sipped a glass of Alkermes, which a servant-man brought in soon afterwards, and then I took my leave. She, however, only allowed me to go, after full assurance that I'd not fail to call the following day.

'On the morrow I was there at the appointed hour. She first made me sit down by the bedside, to rest awhile. She pressed my hand and tenderly patted it—that hand, she said, which had done her so much good, and which was to operate marvelous cures ere long. "Only, doctor," added she, simpering, "the pain has gone higher up."

'I could hardly keep from smiling, and I began to ask myself of what nature this pain was.

'I set myself to rub. From the broad ankle my hand went up to the knee, then higher, and always higher, to her evident satisfaction. When at last it had reached the top of her legs,— "There, there, doctor! you have hit it," she said, in a soft, purring voice; "how clever you are to find the right spot. Rub gently all around there. Yes, like that; neither higher up nor lower down—a little more broadwise, perhaps —just a *leetle* more in the middle, doctor! Oh, what good it does me to be rubbed like that! I feel quite another person; ever so much younger—quite frisky, in fact. Rub, doctor, rub!" And she rolled in the bed rapturously, after the fashion of an old tabby.

'Then, all at once,—"But I think you are mesmerizing me, doctor! Oh, what fine blue eyes you have! I can see myself in your luminous pupils as in a mirror." Thereupon, putting an arm round my neck, she began to pull me down on her, and to kiss me eagerly—or I ought rather to say, to suck me with two thick lips that felt against mine like huge horse-leeches.

'Seeing that I could not go on with my massage, and getting to understand at last what kind of friction she required, I pushed aside the tufts of coarse, crisp, and thick hair, I introduced the tip of my finger between the bulgy lips, and tickled, rubbed, and chafed the full-sized and frisky clitoris in such a way that I soon made it piss copiously; that, however—far from soothing and satisfying her—only titillated and excited her; so that after this there was no escaping from her clutches. She was, moreover, holding me by the right sort of handle, and I could not afford—like Joseph—to run away and leave it in her hand.

'To calm her, therefore, nothing else was left to me but to get on top of her and administer another kind of massage, which I did with as good a grace as I could, although, as you are all aware, I never cared for women, and above all, for stale ones. Still—for a woman and an old one—she was not so bad, after all. Her lips were thick, fleshy, and bulgy; the sphincter had not got relaxed with age, the erectile tissue had lost none of its muscular strength, her grip was powerful, and the pleasure she gave me was not to be despised. I therefore poured two libations into her before I got from over her, during which time she from purring began to mew, and then actually to shriek like a screech-owl, so great was the pleasure she was deriving.

'Whether true or not, she said that she had never felt such pleasure all her life. Anyhow, the cure I effected was a wonderful one, for she shortly afterwards quite recovered the use of her legs. Even N—n was proud of me. It is to her and to my arms that I owe my position as a masseur.'

'Well, and that jewel?' said I.

'Yes, I was quite forgetting it. The summer came, so she had to leave town and go to a watering-place, where I had no wish to follow her; she consequently made me swear that I'd not have a single woman during her absence. I, of course, did so with an easy conscience and a light heart.

'When she came back, she made me take my oath again, after which she unbuttoned my trousers, dragged out Sir Priapus, and in due form crowned him as a *Rosière*.

'I may say, however, that he was not at all stiff-necked and uppish; nay, he seemed so overcome—perhaps he thought he did not deserve this honor—that he bowed down his head quite meekly. I used to wear that jewel on my chain, but everyone kept asking me what it was. I told her of it, and she presented me with this chain and made me wear it round my neck.'

The agape had come to an end, the spiced aphrodisiac dishes, the strong drinks, the merry conversation, stirred up again our sluggish lust. Little by little the position on every couch became more provoking, the jokes more obscene, the songs more lascivious; the mirth was more uproarious, the brains were all aglow, the flesh was tingling with newly-awakened desire. Almost every man was naked, every phallus was stiff and stark; it seemed quite a pandemonium of lewdness.

One of the guests showed us how to make a Priapean fountain, or the proper way of sipping liqueurs. He got a young Ganymede to pour a continuous thread of Chartreuse out of a long-beaked silver ewer down on Briancourt's chest. The liquid trickled down the stomach and through the tiny curls of the jet-black, rose-scented hair, all along the phallus, and into the mouth of the man kneeling in front of him. The three men were so handsome, the group so classic, that a photograph was taken of it by limelight.

'It's very pretty,' said the Spahi, 'but I think I can show you something better still.'

'And what is that?' asked Briancourt.

'The way they eat preserved dates stuffed with pistachioes in Algiers; and as you happen to have some on the table, we can try it.'

The old general chuckled, evidently enjoying the fun.

The Spahi then made his bedfellow go on all fours, with his head down and his backside up; then he carefully placed the dates where he wanted them.

'Wait, don't get up yet,' said the Spahi, 'I haven't yet quite finished; let me just put the fruit of the tree of knowledge into it.' Thereupon he got on him, and taking his instrument in his hand, he pressed it into the hole in which the dates had been; and slippery as the gap was, it disappeared entirely after a thrust or two.

At the sight of this *tableau vivant* of hellish concupiscence, all our blood rose bubbling to our heads. Everyone seemed eager to enjoy what those men were feeling. Every unhooded phallus was not only full of blood, but as stiff as a rod of iron, and painful in its erection. Everyone was writhing as if tormented by an inward convulsion. I myself, not inured to such sights, was groaning with pleasure, maddened by Teleny's exciting kisses, and by the doctor, who was pressing his lips on the soles of my feet.

Finally, by the lusty thrusts the Spahi was now giving, we understood that the last moment had come. It was like an electric shock amongst us all.

'They enjoy, they enjoy!' was the cry, uttered from every lip.

All the couples were cleaving together, kissing each other, rubbing their naked bodies one against the other, trying what new excess their lechery could devise.

When at last the Spahi pulled his limp organ out, the sodomized man fell senseless on the couch, all covered with perspiration.

'Ah!' said the Spahi, quietly lighting a cigarette, 'what pleasures can be compared with those of the Cities of the Plain? The Arabs are right. They are our masters in this art; for there, if every man is not passive in his manhood, he is always so in early youth and in old age, when he cannot be active any longer. They —unlike ourselves—know by long practice how to prolong this pleasure for an everlasting time. Their instruments are not huge, but they swell out to goodly proportions. They are skilled in enhancing their own pleasure by the satisfaction they afford to others. They do not flood you with watery sperm, they squirt on you a few thick drops that burn you like fire. How smooth and glossy their skin is! What a lava is bubbling in their veins! They are not men, they are lions; and they roar to lusty purpose.'

'You must have tried a good many, I suppose?'

'Scores of them; I enlisted for that, and I must say I did enjoy myself. Why, Viscount, your implement would only tickle me agreeably, if you could only keep it stiff long enough.'

Then pointing to a broad flask that stood on the table, 'Why, that bottle there could, I think, be easily thrust in me, and only give me pleasure.'

'Will you try?' said many voices.

'Why not?'

'No, you had better not,' warned Dr. Charles, who had crept by my side.

'Why, what is there to be afraid of?'

'It is a crime against nature,' said the physician, smiling.

'In fact, it would be worse than buggery, it would be bottlery,' laughed Briancourt.

For all answer the Spahi threw himself face upwards on the ledge of the couch, with his bum uplifted towards us. Then two men went and sat on either side, so that he might rest his legs on their shoulders.

'Who will have the goodness to moisten and lubricate the edges a little?'

Many seemed anxious to give themselves that pleasure, but it was allotted to one who had modestly introduced himself as a *maitre de langues*, 'although with my proficiency' — he added — 'I might well call myself professor in the noble art.' He was indeed a man who bore the weight of a great name, not only of old lineage—never sullied by any plebeian blood—but also famous in war, statesmanship, in literature and in science. He went on his knees before that mass of flesh, usually called an arse, pointed his tongue like a lance-head, and darted it in.

'Now,' said he, with the pride of an artist who has just finished his work, 'my task is done.'

Another person had taken the bottle, and had rubbed it over with the grease of a *paté de foie gras*, then he began to press it in.

'Aie, aie!' said the Spahi, biting his lips; 'it is a tight fit, but it's in at last.'

'Am I hurting you?'

'It did pain a little, but now it's all over'; and he began to groan with pleasure.

The Spahi's face expressed a mixture of acute pain and intense lechery; all the nerves of his body seemed stretched and quivering, as if under the action of a strong battery; his eyes were half closed, and the pupils had almost disappeared, his clenched teeth were gnashed, as the bottle was, every now and then, thrust a little further in. His phallus, which had been limp and lifeless when he had felt nothing but pain, was again acquiring its full proportions; then all the veins in it began to swell, the nerves to stiffen themselves to their utmost.

'Do you want to be kissed?' asked someone, seeing how the rod was shaking.

'Thanks,' he said, 'I feel enough as it is.'

'What is it like?'

'A sharp and yet an agreeable irritation from my bum up to my brain.'

In fact his whole body was convulsed, as the bottle went slowly in and out, ripping and almost quartering him.

The hand of the manipulator was convulsed. He gave the bottle a strong shake.

We were all breathless with excitement, seeing the intense pleasure the Spahi was feeling, when all at once, amidst the perfect silence that followed each of the soldier's groans, a slight shivering sound was heard, which was at once succeeded by a loud scream of pain and terror from the prostrate man, of horror from the other. The bottle had broken; the handle and part of it came out, cutting all the flesh that pressed against it, the other part remained engulfed within the anus.

8

Time passed—

—Of course, time never stops, so it is useless to say that it passed. Tell me, rather, what became of the poor Spahi?

—He died, poor fellow! At first there was a general *sauve qui peut* from Briancourt's. Dr. Charles sent for his instruments and extracted the pieces of glass, and I was told that the poor young man suffered the most excruciating pains like a Stoic without uttering a cry or a groan; his courage was indeed worthy of a better cause. The operation finished, Dr. Charles told the sufferer that he ought to be transported to the hospital, for he was afraid that an inflammation might take place in the pierced parts of the intestines.

'What!' said he; 'go to the hospital, and expose myself to the sneers of all the nurses and doctors—never!'

'But,' said his friend, 'should inflammation set in—'

'It would be all up with me?'

'I am afraid so.'

'And is it likely that the inflammation will take place?'

'Alas! more than likely.'

'And if it does—?'

Dr. Charles looked serious, but gave no answer.

'It might be fatal?'

'Yes.'

'Well, I'll think it over. Anyhow, I must go home—that is, to my lodgings, to put some things to rights.'

In fact, he was accompanied home, and there he begged to be left alone for half an hour.

As soon as he was by himself, he locked the door of the room, took a revolver and shot himself. The cause of the suicide remained a mystery to everybody except ourselves.

This, and another case which happened shortly afterwards, cast a dampness on us all, and for some time put an end to Briancourt's symposiums.

—And what was this other case?

—One you have most likely read about, for it was in all the papers at the time it occurred. An elderly gentleman, whose name I have quite forgotten, was silly enough to be caught in the very act of sodomizing a soldier—a lusty young recruit lately arrived from the country. The case made a great ado, for the gentleman occupied a foremost position in society, and was, moreover, not only a person of unblemished reputation, but a most religious man besides.

—What! do you think it possible for a truly religious man to be addicted to such a vice?

—Of course it is. Vice renders us superstitious; and what is superstition save an obsolete and discarded form of worship. It is the sinner and not the saint that needs a Saviour, an intercessor, and a priest; if you have nothing to atone for, what is the use of religion to you? Religion is no bridle to a passion, which — though termed against nature—is so deeply engrafted in our nature that reason can neither cool nor mask it. The Jesuits are, therefore, the only real priests. Far from damning you, like ranting dissenters do, they have at least a thousand palliations for all the diseases which they cannot cure — a balm for every heavy-laden conscience.

But to return to our story. When the young soldier was asked by the judge how he could thus degrade himself, and sully the uniform he wore,—'M. le Juge,' quoth he, ingenuously, 'the gentleman was very kind to me. Moreover, being a very influential person, he promised me *un avancement dans le corps'* (*an advancement in the body*)!

Time passed, and I lived happily with Teleny —for who would not have been happy with him, handsome, good, and clever as he was? His playing now was so genial, so exuberant with lusty life, so beaming with sensual happiness, that he was daily becoming a greater favorite, and all the ladies were more than ever in love with him; but what did I care, was he not wholly mine?

—What! you were not jealous?

—How could I be jealous, when he never gave me the slightest cause. I had the key of his house, and could go there at any moment of the day or night. If he ever left town I invariably accompanied him. No, I was sure of his love, and therefore of his fidelity, as he likewise had perfect faith in me.

He had, however, one great defect—he was an artist, and had an artist's lavishness in the composition of his character. Although he now gained enough to live comfortably, his concerts did not yet afford him the means to live in the princely way he did. I often lectured him on that score; he invariably promised me not to throw away his money, but alas! there was in the web of his nature some of the yarn of which my namesake's mistress — Manon Lescaut — was made.

Knowing that he had debts, and that he was often worried with duns, I begged him several

times to give me his accounts, that I might settle all his bills, and allow him to begin life
afresh. He would not have me even speak of
such a thing.

'I know myself,' he said, 'better than you do;
if I accept once, I'll do so again, and what will
be the upshot? I'll end by being kept by you.'

'And where is the great harm?' was my reply. 'Do you think I'd love you less for it?'

'Oh! no; you perhaps might love me even
more on account of the money I cost you—for
we are often fond of a friend according to
what we do for him—but I might be induced
to love you less; gratitude is such an unbearable
burden to human nature. I am your lover, it is
true, but do not let me sink lower than that,
Camille,' he said, with a wistful eagerness.

'See! since I knew you, have I not tried to
make ends meet? Some day or other I might
even manage to pay off old debts; so do not
tempt me any more.'

Thereupon, taking me in his arms, he covered
me with kisses.

How handsome he was just then! I think I
can see him, leaning on a dark-blue satin cush-
ion, with his arms under his head, as you are
leaning now, for you have many of his feline,
graceful ways.

We had become inseparable, for our love
seemed to wax stronger every day, and with
us 'fire never drove out fire,' but, on the contrary, it grew on what it fed; so I lived far
more with him than at home.

My office did not take up much of my time, and I only remained there just long enough to attend to my business, and also to leave him some moments to practice. The remainder of the day we were together.

At the theatre we occupied the same box, alone, or with my mother. Neither of us accepted, as was soon known, any invitation to whatsoever entertainment where the other was not also a guest. At the public promenades we either walked, rode or drove together. In fact, had our union been blessed by the Church, it could not have been a closer one. Let the moralist after that explain to me the harm we did, or the law-giver that would apply to us the penalty inflicted to the worst of criminals, the wrong we did to society.

Although we did not dress alike, still—being almost of the same build, of about the same age, as well as of identical tastes—the people, who saw us always arm-in-arm, ended by not being able to think of the one apart from the other.

Our friendship had become almost proverbial, and 'No René without Camille' had become a kind of by-word.

—But you, that had been so terrorized by the anonymous note, did you not fear that people might begin to suspect the real nature of your attachment?

—That fear had quite passed away. Does the shame of a divorce-court keep the adulteress from meeting her lover? Do the impending terrors of the law keep the thief from stealing? My conscience had been lulled by happiness into a calm repose; moreover, the knowledge I had acquired at Briancourt's gatherings, that I was not the only member of our cankered society who loved in the Socratic fashion, and that men of the highest intelligence, of the kindest heart, and of the purest aesthetic feelings, were—like myself—sodomists, quieted me. It is not the pains of hell we dread, but rather the low society we might meet there below.

The ladies now had, I believe, begun to suspect that our excessive friendship was of too loving a nature; and as I have heard since, we had been nicknamed the angels of Sodom—hinting, thereby, that these heavenly messengers had not escaped their doom. But what did I care if some tribades suspected us of sharing their own frailties.

—And your mother?

—She was actually suspected of being René's mistress. I was amused by it; the idea was so very absurd.

—But had she not any inkling of your love for your friend?

—You know the husband is always the last to suspect his wife's infidelity. She was surprised to see the change wrought in me. She even asked me how it was that I had learned to like the man I had snubbed and treated with such disdain; and then she added:

'You see you must never be prejudiced, and judge people without knowing them.'

A circumstance, however, which happened at that time forcibly diverted my mother's attention away from Teleny.

A young ballet-girl, whose attention I had apparently attracted at a masked ball, either feeling a certain liking for me, or else thinking me an easy prey, wrote a most loving epistle to me, and invited me to call upon her.

Not knowing how to refuse the honor she was conferring upon me, and at the same time never liking to treat any woman scornfully, I sent her a huge basket of flowers and a book explaining their meaning.

She understood that my love was bestowed elsewhere; still, in return for my present, I received a fine large photograph of her. I then called on her to thank her, and thus we soon got to be very good friends, but only friends and nothing more.

As I had left the letter and the portrait in my room, my mother, who certainly saw the one, must likewise have seen the other, too. That is why she never gave my *liaison* with the musician a single thought.

In her conversation there were, every now and then, either slight innuendoes or broad hints about the folly of men who ruin themselves for the *corps de ballet,* or about the bad taste of those who marry their own and other people's mistresses, but that was all.

She knew that I was my own master, therefore she did not meddle with my own private life, but left me to do exactly what I liked. If I had a *faux ménage* somewhere or other, so much the better or so much the worse for me. She was glad that I had the good taste to respect *les convenances,* and not to make a public affair of it. Only a man of forty-five who had made up his mind not to marry can brave public opinion, and keep a mistress ostentatiously.

Moreover, it has occurred to me that, as she did not wish me to look too closely into the aim of her frequent little journeys, she left me full liberty to act at my own discretion.

—She was still a young woman at that time, was she not?

—That entirely depends upon what you call a young woman. She was about thirty-seven or thirty-eight, and was exceedingly young-looking for her age. She has always been spoken of as a most beautiful and desirable woman.

She was very handsome. Tall, with splendid arms and shoulders, a well-poised and erect head, you could not have helped remarking her whithersoever she went. Her eyes were large and of an invariable and impassable calmness that nothing ever seemed to ruffle; her eyebrows, which almost met, were level and thick; her hair dark, naturally wavy, and in massy clusters; her forehead, low and broad; her nose, straight and small. All this combined to give something classically grave and statuesque to her whole countenance.

Her mouth, however, was her best feature; not only was it perfect in its outline, but her almost pouting lips were so cherry-like, sappy, and luscious, that you longed to taste them. Such a mouth must have played the deuce with the men of strong desires who looked upon it—nay, it must have acted like a love-philter, a-wakening the eager fire of lust even in the most sluggish hearts. In fact, few were the trousers that did not swell out in my mother's presence, notwithstanding all their owner's efforts not to show the tattoo which was being beaten within them; and this, I should think, is the finest compliment that can be paid to a woman's beauty, for it is a natural not a maudlin one.

Her manners, however, had that repose, and her gait that calmness, which not only stamp the caste of Vere de Vere but which characterize an Italian peasant and a French *grande dame*, though never met with in the German aristocracy. She seemed born to reign as a queen of drawing-rooms, and therefore accepted as her due, and without the slightest show of pleasure, not only all the flattering articles of the fashionable papers, but also the respectful homage of a host of distant admirers, not one of whom would have dared to attempt a flirtation with her. To everybody she was like Juno, an irreproachable woman who might have been either a volcano or an iceberg.

—And may I ask what she was?

—A lady who received and paid innumerable visits, and who seemed always to preside everywhere — at the dinner-parties she gave, and also at those she accepted—therefore the paragon of a lady patroness. A shopkeeper once observed, 'It is a red-letter day when Madame Des Grieux stops before our windows, for she not only attracts the gentlemen's attention, but also that of the ladies, who often buy what has caught her artistic eye.'

She had, besides, that excellent thing in woman:

> *Her voice was ever soft,*
> *Gentle and low;*

for I think I could get accustomed to a plain-featured wife, but not to one whose voice is shrill, harsh, and piercing.

—They say that you looked very much like her.

—Do they? Anyhow, I hope that you do not wish me to praise my mother like Lamartine did, and then to add modestly, 'I am after her own image.'

But how is it that having become a widow so young, she did not maarry again? Rich and handsome as she was, she must have had as many suitors as Penelope herself.

—Some day or other I will tell you her life, and then you will understand why she preferred her liberty to the ties of matrimony.

—She was fond of you, was she not?

—Yes, very; and so was I of her. Moreover —had I not been given to those propensities which I dared not avow to her, and which only tribades can understand; had I, like other men of my age, been living a merry life of fornication with whores, mistresses, and lively *grisettes*—I should often have made her the confidante of my erotic exploits, for in the moment of bliss our prodigal feelings are often blunted by the too great excess, while the remembrance doled out at our will is a real twofold pleasure of the senses and of the mind.

Teleny, however, had of late become a kind of bar between us, and I think she had got to be rather jealous of him, for his name seemed to have become as objectionable to her as it formerly had been to me.

— Did she begin to suspect your *liaison?*

— I did not know whether she suspected it, or if she was beginning to be jealous of the affection I bore him.

Matters, however, were coming to a crisis, and were shaping towards the dreadful way in which they ended.

One day a grand concert was to be given at B—, and L—, who was to play, having been taken ill, Teleny was asked to take his place. It was an honor he could not refuse.

'I am loath to leave you,' said he, 'even for a day or two, for I know that just now you are so busy that you cannot possibly get away, especially as your manager is ill.'

'Yes,' said I, 'it is rather awkward, still I might—'

'No, no, it would be foolish; I'll not allow you.'

'But you know it is so long since you played

at a concert where I was not present,' I said.

'You'll be present in mind if not in body. I shall see you sitting in your usual place, and I shall play for you and you alone. Besides, we have never been parted for any length of time —no, not for a single day since Briancourt's letter. Let us try and see if we can live apart for two days. Who knows? Perhaps, sometime or other—'

'What do you mean?'

'Nothing, only you might get tired of this life. You might, like other men, marry just to have a family.'

'A family!' I burst out laughing. 'Is that encumbrance so very necessary to a man's happiness?'

'My love might surfeit you.'

'René, don't speak in that way! Could I live without you?'

He smiled incredulously.

'What! do you doubt my love?'

'Can I doubt that the stars are fire? but,' he continued slowly, and looking at me, 'do you doubt mine?'

It seemed to me as if he had grown pale when he put that question to me.

'No. Have you ever given me the slightest cause to doubt it?'

'And if I were unfaithful?'

'Teleny,' said I, feeling faint, 'you have another lover.' And I saw him in the arms of someone else, tasting that bliss which was mine and mine alone.

'No,' he said, 'I have not; but if I had?'

'You would love him—or her, and then my life would be blasted forever.'

'No, not forever; only for a time, perhaps. But could you not forgive me?'

'Yes, if you still loved me.'

The idea of losing him sent a sharp pang through my heart, which seemed to act like a sound flagellation, my eyes were filled with tears, and my blood was on fire. I therefore clasped him in my arms and hugged him, straining all my muscles in my embrace; my lips eagerly sought his, my tongue was in his mouth. The more I kissed him the sadder I grew, and the more eager was my desire. I stopped a moment to look at him. How handsome he was that day! His beauty was almost ethereal.

I can see him now with that aureole of hair so soft and silky, the color of a golden ray of sunshine playing through a crystal goblet of topaz-colored wine, with his moist half-opened mouth, oriental in its voluptuousness, with his blood-red lips which no illness had withered like those of the painted, mush-scented courtesans who sell a few moments of carrion bliss for gold, nor discolored like those of pale, wasp-waisted, anemic virgins, whose monthly menses have left in their veins nothing but a colorless fluid instead of ruby blood.

And those luminous eyes, in which an innate, sullen fire seemed to temper the lust of the carnal mouth, just as his cheeks, almost child-like in their innocent, peachy roundness, con-

trasted with the massive throat so full of man-
ly vigor—

> *and a form indeed.*
> *Where every god did seem to set his seal*
> *To give the world assurance of a man.*

Let the listless, orris-scented aesthete in love
with a shadow, scourge me after this for the
burning, maddening passion which his virile
beauty excited in my breast. Well—yes, I am
like the men of fervent blood born on the vol-
canic soil of Naples, or under the glowing sun
of the East; and, after all, I would rather be
like Brunette Latun—a man who loved his fel-
low-men—than like Dante, who sent them all
to hell, while he himself went to that effete
place called heaven, with a languid vision of
his own creation.

Teleny returned my kisses with the passionate eagerness of despair. His lips were on fire,
his love seemed to have changed into a raging
fever. I don't know what had come over me,
but I felt that pleasure could kill, but not calm
me. My head was all aglow!

There are two kinds of lascivious feelings,
both equally strong and overpowering: the one
is the fervent, carnal lust of the senses, en-
kindled in the genital organs and mounting to
the brain, making human beings

> *Swim in mirth, and fancy that they feel*
> *Divinity within them breeding wings*
> *Wherewith to scorn the earth.*

The other is the cold libidinousness of fancy, the keen and gall-like irradiation of the brain which parches the healthy blood

as with new wine intoxicated,

The first, the strong concupiscence of lusty youth—natural to the flesh, is satisfied as soon as men take largely

their fill of love and love's disport,

and the heavily-laden anther has sturdily shaken forth the seed that clogged it; and then they feel as our first parents did, when dewy sleep

Oppressed them, wearied with their amorous play.

The body then so delightfully light seems to rest on 'earth's freshest, softest lap,' and the slothful yet half-awakened mind broods over its slumbering shell.

The second, kindled in the head,

bred of unkindly fumes,

is the lechery of senility—a morbid craving, like the hunger of surfeited gluttony. The senses, like Messalina,

lassata sed non satiata,

ever tingling, keep hankering after the impossible. The spermatic ejaculations, far from calming the body, only irritate it, for the exciting influence of a salacious fancy continues after the anther has yielded all its seed. Even if acrid blood comes instead of the balmy, creamlike fluid, it brings with it nothing but a painful irritation. If, unlike as in satyriasis, an erection does not take place, and the phallus remains limp and lifeless, still the nervous system is no less convulsed by impotent desire and lechery—a mirage of the over-heated brain, no less shattering because it is effete.

These two feelings combined together are something akin to what I underwent as, holding Teleny clasped against my throbbing, heaving breast, I felt within me the contagion of his eager longing, and of his overpowering sadness.

I had taken off my friend's shirt collar and cravat to see and to feel his beautiful bare neck, then little by little I stripped him of all his clothes, till at last he remained naked in my embrace.

What a model of voluptuous comeliness he was, with his strong and muscular shoulders, his broad and swelling chest, his skin of a pearly whiteness, as soft and as fresh as the petals of a waterlily, his limbs rounded like those of Leotard, with whom every woman was in love. His thighs, his legs and feet in their exquisite grace, were perfect models.

The more I looked upon him the more en-amored I was of him. But the sight was not enough. I had to heighten the visual delight by the sense of touch, I had to feel the tough and yet elastic muscles of the arm in the palm of my hand, to fondle his massive and sinewy breast, to paddle his back. From there my hands descended down to the round lobes of the rump, and I clasped him against me by the buttocks. Thereupon, tearing off my clothes, I pressed all his body on mine, and rubbed against him, wriggling like a worm. Lying over him as I was, my tongue was in his mouth, searching for his, that receded, and was darted out when mine retired, for they seemed to play a wanton, bickering game of hide-and-seek together—a game which made all the body quiver with delight.

Then our fingers twisted the crisp and curly hair that grew all around the middle parts, or handled the testicles, so softly and so gently that they were hardly sentient of the touch, and still they shivered in a way that almost made the fluid in them flow out before its time.

The most skilled of prostitutes could never give such thrilling sensations as those which I felt with my lover, for the tweake is, after all, only acquainted with the pleasures she herself has felt; while the keener emotions, not being those of her sex, are unknown to her and can-not be imagined by her.

Likewise, no man is ever able to madden a

woman with such overpowering lust as another tribade can, for she alone knows how to tickle her on the right spot just in the nick of time. The quintessence of bliss can, therefore, only be enjoyed by beings of the same sex.

Our two bodies were now in as close a contact as the glove is to the hand it sheaves, our feet were tickling each other wantonly, our knees were pressed together, the skin of our thighs seemed to cleave and to form one flesh.

Though I was loath to rise, still, feeling his stiff and swollen phallus throbbing against my body, I was just going to tear myself off from him, and to take his fluttering implement of pleasure in my mouth and drain it, when he— feeling that mine was not only turgid, but moist and brimful to overflowing—clasped me with his arms and kept me down.

Opening his thighs, he thereupon took my legs between his own, and entwined them in such a way that his heels pressed against the side of my calves. For a moment I was gripped as in a vise, and I could hardly move.

Then, loosening his arms, he uplifted himself, placed a pillow under his buttocks, which were thus well apart—his legs being all the time widely open.

Having done this, he took hold of my rod and pressed it against his gaping anus. The tip of the frisky phallus soon found its entrance in the hospitable hole that endeavored to give it admission. I pressed a little; the whole of the glans was engulfed. The sphincter soon gripped it in such a way that it could not come out without an effort. I thrust it slowly to prolong as much as possible the ineffable sensation that ran through every limb, to calm the quivering nerves, and to allay the heat of the blood. Another push, and half the phallus was in his body. I pulled it out half an inch, though it seemed to me a yard by the prolonged pleasure I felt. I pressed forward again, and the whole of it, down to its very root, was all swallowed up. Thus wedged, I vainly endeavored to drive it higher up—an impossible feat, and, clasped as I was, I felt it wriggling in its sheath like a baby in its mother's womb, giving myself and him an unutterable and delightful titillation.

So keen was the bliss that overcame me, that I asked myself if some ethereal, life-giving fluid were not being poured on my head, and trickling down slowly over my quivering flesh?

Surely the rain-awakened flowers must be conscious of such a sensation during a shower, after they have been parched by the scorching rays of an estival sun.

Teleny again put his arm round me and held me tight. I gazed at myself within his eyes, he saw himself in mine. During this voluptuous, lambent feeling, we patted each other's bodies softly, our lips cleaved together and my tongue was again in his mouth. We remained in this copulation almost without stirring, for I felt that the slightest movement would provoke a copious ejaculation, and this feeling was too exquisite to be allowed to pass away so quickly. Still we could not help writhing, and we almost swooned away with delight. We were both shivering with lust, from the roots of our hair to the tips of our toes; all the flesh of our bodies kept bickering luxuriously, just as placid waters of the mere do at noontide when kissed by the sweet-scented, wanton breeze that has just deflowered the virgin rose.

Such intensity of delight could not, however, last very long; a few almost unwilling contractions of the sphincter brandled the phallus, and then the first brunt was over; I thrust in with might and main, I wallowed in him; my breath came thickly; I panted, I sighed, I groaned. The thick burning fluid was spouted out slowly and at long intervals.

As I rubbed myself against him, he underwent all the sensations I was feeling; for I was hardly drained of the last drop before I was likewise bathed with his own seething sperm. We did not kiss each other any further; our languid, half-open, lifeless lips only aspired each other's breath. Our sightless eyes saw each other no more, for we fell into that divine prostration which follows shattering ecstasy.

Oblivion, however, did not follow, but we remained in a benumbed state of torpor, speechless, forgetting everything except the love we bore each other, unconscious of everything save the pleasure of feeling each other's bodies, which, however, seemed to have lost their own individuality, mingled and confounded as they were together. Apparently we had but one head and one heart, for they beat in such unison, and the same vague thoughts flitted through both our brains.

Why did not Jehovah strike us dead that moment? Had we not provoked Him enough? How was it that the jealous God was not envious of our bliss? Why did He not hurl one of his avenging thunderbolts at us, and annihilate us?

— What! and have pitched you both headlong into hell?

— Well, what then? Hell, of course, is no excelsior—no place of false aspirations after an unreachable ideal of fallacious hopes and bitter disappointments. Never pretending to be what we are not, we shall find there true contentedness of mind, and our bodies will be able to develop those faculties with which nature has endowed them. Not being either hypocrites or dissemblers, the dread of being seen such as we really are can never torment us.

If we are grossly bad, we shall at least be truthfully so. There will be amongst us that honesty which here on earth exists only amongst thieves; and moreover, we shall have that genial companionship of fellow-beings after our own heart.

Is hell, then, such a place to be dreaded? Thus, even admitting of an afterlife in the bottomless pit, which I do not, hell would only be the paradise of those whom nature has created fit for it. Do animals repine for not having been created men? No, I think not. Why should we, then, make ourselves unhappy for not having been born angels?

At that moment it seemed as if we were floating somewhere between heaven and earth, not thinking that everything that has a beginning has likewise an end.

The senses were blunted, so that the downy couch upon which we were resting was like a bed of clouds. A deathlike silence was reigning around us. The very noise and hum of the great city seemed to have stopped—or, at least, we did not hear it. Could the earth have stopped in its rotation, and the hand of Time have arrested itself in its dismal march?

I remember languidly wishing that my life could pass away in that placidly dull and dreamy state, so like a mesmeric trance, when the benumbed body is thrown into a death-like torpor, and the mind,

Like an ember among fallen ashes,

is just wakeful enough to feel the consciousness of ease and of peaceful rest.

All at once we were roused from our pleasant somnolence by the jarring sound of an electric bell.

Teleny jumped up, hastened to wrap himself in a dressing-gown, and to attend to the summons. A few moments afterward he came back with a telegram in his hand.

'What is it?' I asked.

'A message from—,' he replied, looking at

me wistfully, and with a certain trepidation in his voice.

'And you have to go?'

'I suppose I must,' said he, with a mournful sadness in his eyes.

'Is it so distasteful to you?'

'Distasteful is not the word; it is unbearable. This is the first parting, and—'

'Yes, but only for a day or two.'

'A day or two,' added he, gloomily, 'is the space that divides life from death:

> *It is the little rift within the lute,*
> *That by-and-by will make the music mute,*
> *And ever widening slowly silence all.'*

'Teleny, you have had for some days a weight on your mind—something that I cannot fathom. Will you not tell your friend what it is?'

He opened his eyes widely, as if he were looking into the depths of limitless space, while a painful expression was seen upon his lips; and then he added slowly:

'My fate. Have you forgotten the prophetic vision you had that evening of the charity concert?'

'What! Adrian mourning over dead Antinous?'

'Yes.'

'A fancy bred in my over-heated brain by the conflicting qualities of your Hungarian music, so stirringly sensuous and at the same time so gorgeously mournful.'

He shook his head sadly.

'No, it was something more than idle fancy.'

'A change has been taking place in you, Teleny. Perhaps it is the religious or spiritual element of your nature that is predominating just now over the sensual, but you are not what you were.'

'I feel that I have been too happy, but that our happiness is built on sand—a bond like ours—'

'Not blessed by the Church, repugnant to the nice feelings of most men.'

'Well—yes, in such a love there is always

A little pitted speck in garnered fruit
That, rotting inward, slowly smothers all.

Why did we meet—or, rather, why was not one of us born a woman? Had you only been some poor girl—'

'Come, leave aside your morbid fancies, and tell me candidly if you would have loved me more than you do.'

He looked at me sadly, but could not bring himself to utter an untruth. Still, after a while he added, sighing:

'There is a love that is to last,
When the hot days of youth are past.

Tell me, Camille, is such love ours?'

'Why not? Can you not always be as fond of me as I am of you, or do I only care for you on account of the sensual pleasures you afford me?

You know that my heart yearns for you when the senses are satiated and the desire is blunted.'

'Still, had it not been for me, you might have loved some woman whom you could have married—'

'And have found out, but too late, that I was born with other cravings. No, sooner or later I should have followed my destiny.'

'Now it might be quite different; satiated with my love, you might, perhaps, marry and forget me.'

'Never. But come, have you been confessing yourself? Are you going to turn Calvinist? or, like the "Dame aux Camélias," or Antinous, do you think it necessary to sacrifice yourself on the altar of love for my sake?'

'Please, don't joke.'

'No, I'll tell you what we'll do. Let us leave France. Let us go to Spain, to Southern Italy —nay, let us leave Europe, and go to the East, where I must surely have lived during some former life, and which I have a hankering to see, just as if the land

Where the flowers ever blossom, the beams ever shine,

had been the home of my youth; there, unknown to everyone, forgotten by the world.'

'Yes, but can I leave this town?' he said.

I knew that of late Teleny had been dunned a good deal, and that his life had often been rendered unpleasant by usurers.

Caring, therefore, but little what people might think of me—besides, who has not a good opinion of the man that pays?—I had called all his creditors together, and, unknown to him, I had settled all his debts. I was about to tell him so, and relieve him from the weight that was oppressing him, when Fate—blind, inexorable, crushing Fate—sealed my mouth.

There was again a loud ring at the door. Had that bell been rung a few seconds later, how different his life and mine would have been! But it was *Kismet,* as the Turks say.

It was the carriage that had come to take him to the station. While he was getting ready, I helped him to pack up his dress suit and some other little things he might require. I took up, by chance, a small matchbox containing French letters, and smiling, said:

'Here, I'll put them in your trunk; they might be useful.'

He shuddered, and grew deathly pale.

'Who knows?' said I; 'some beautiful lady patroness—'

'Please, don't joke,' he retorted, almost angrily.

'Oh! now I can afford to do so, but once—do you know that I was even jealous of my mother?'

Teleny at that moment dropped the mirror he was holding, which, as it fell, was shivered to pieces.

For a moment we both looked aghast. Was it not a dreadful omen?

Just then the clock on the mantelpiece struck the hour. Teleny shrugged his shoulders.

'Come,' he said, 'there's no time to lose.'

He snatched up his portmanteau, and we hurried downstairs.

I accompanied him to the terminus, and before leaving him when he alighted from the carriage, my arms were clasped around him, and our lips met in a last and lingering kiss. They clung fondly to one another, not with the fever of lust, but with a love all fraught with tenderness, and with a sorrow that gripped the muscles of the heart.

His kiss was like the last emanation of a withering flower, or like the sweet scent shed at evening tide by one of those delicate white cactus blossoms that open their petals at dawn, follow the sun in its diurnal march, then droop and fade away with the planet's last rays.

At parting from him I felt as if I had been bereft of my soul itself. My love was like a Nessus shirt, the severing of which was as painful as having my flesh torn from me piecemeal. It was as if the joy of my life had been snatched away from me.

I watched him as he hurried away with his springy step and feline grace. When he had reached the portal he turned round. He was deathly pale, and in his despair he looked like a man about to commit suicide. He waved a last farewell, and quickly disappeared.

The sun had set for me. Night had come over the world. I felt

like a soul belated;
In hell and heaven unmated;

and, shuddering, I asked myself, what morn would come out of all this darkness?

The agony visible on his face struck a deep terror within me; then I thought how foolish we both were in giving each other such unnecessary pain, and I rushed out of the carriage after him.

All at once a heavy country lout ran up against me, and clasped me in his arms.

'Oh,—!' I did not catch the name he said—'what an unexpected pleasure! How long have you been here?'

'Let me go—let me go! You are mistaken!' I screamed out, but he held me fast.

As I wrestled with the man, I heard the signal bell ring. With a strong jerk I pushed him away, and ran into the station. I reached the platform a few seconds too late, the train was in motion, Teleny had disappeared.

Nothing was then left for me to do but to post a letter to this friend of mine, begging him to forgive me for having done what he had often forbidden me to do; that is, to have given an order to my attorney to collect all his outstanding accounts, and pay all those debts that had so long been weighing upon him. That letter, however, he never got.

I jumped back into the cab, and was whirled

away to my office through the crowded thoroughfares of the town.

What a jarring bustle there was everywhere! How sordid and meaningless this world appeared!

A garishly-dressed, smirking female was casting lewd glances at a lad, and tempting him to follow her. A one-eyed satyr was ogling a very young girl—a mere child. I thought I knew him. Yes, it was that loathsome school fellow of mine, Bion, only he looked even more of a pimp than his father used to look. A fat, sleek-headed man was carrying a *cantaloup* melon, and his mouth seemed to be watering at the prospect of the pleasure he would have in eating it after the soup, with his wife and children. I asked myself if ever man or woman could have kissed that slobbering mouth without feeling sick?

I had during these last three days quite neglected my office, and my manager was ill. I therefore felt it my duty to set to work and do what had to be done. Nothwithstanding the sorrow gnawing in my heart, I began answering letters and telegrams, or giving the necessary directions as to how they were to be answered. I worked feverishly, rather like a machine than a man. For a few hours I was quite absorbed in complicated commercial transactions, and although I worked and reckoned clearly, still my friend's face, with his mournful eyes, his voluptuous mouth with its bitter smile, was ever before me, while an aftertaste of his kiss lingered on my lips.

The hour for shutting up the office came, and yet not half of my task was done. I saw, as in a dream, the rueful faces of my clerks kept back from their dinners or from their pleasures. They had all somewhere to go to. I was alone, even my mother was away. I therefore bade them go, saying I should remain with the head bookkeeper. They did not wait to be told twice; in a twinkling the offices were empty.

As for the accountant, he was a commercial fossil, a kind of living calculating machine; grown so old in the office that all his limbs creaked like rusty hinges every time he moved, so that he hardly ever did move. Nobody had ever seen him anywhere else but on his high stool; he was always at his place before any of the junior clerks came in, he was still there when they went off. Life for him had only one aim—that of making endless additions.

Feeling rather sick, I sent the office boy for a bottle of dry sherry and a box of vanilla-wafers. When the lad returned I told him he could go.

I poured out a glass of wine for the bookkeeper, and handed him the box of biscuits. The old man took up the glass with his parchment-colored hand, and held it up to the light as if he were calculating its chemical properties or its specific weight. Then he sipped it slowly with evident gusto.

As for the wafer he looked at it carefully, just as if it had been a draft he was going to register.

Then we both set to work again, and at about ten, all the letters and dispatches having been answered, I heaved a deep sigh of relief.

'If my manager comes tomorrow, as he said he would, he'll be satisfied with me.'

I smiled as this thought flitted through my brain. What was I working for? Lucre, to please my clerk, or for the work itself? I am sure I hardly knew. I think I labored for the feverish excitement the work gave me, just as men play at chess to keep their brains active with other thoughts than those that oppress them; or, perhaps, because I was born with working propensities like bees or ants.

Not wanting to keep the poor bookkeeper on his stool any longer, I admitted the fact to him that it was time to shut up the office. He got up slowly, with a crepitating sound, took off his spectacles like an automaton, wiped them leisurely, put them in their case, quietly took out another pair—for he had glasses for every occasion—put them on his nose, then looked at me.

'You have gone through a vast amount of work. If your grandfather and your father could have seen you, they surely would have been pleased with you.'

I again poured out two glasses of wine, one of which I handed to him. He quaffed the wine, pleased, not with the wine itself, but for my kindness in offering it to him. Then I shook hands with him, and we parted.

Where was I to go now—home?

I wished my mother had come back. I had got a letter from her that very afternoon; in it she said that, instead of returning in a day or two, as she had intended doing, she might, perhaps, go off to Italy for a short time. She was suffering from a slight attack of bronchitis, and she dreaded the fogs and dampness of our town.

Poor mother! I now thought that, since my intimacy with Teleny, there had been a slight estrangement between us; not that I loved her less, but because Teleny engrossed all my mental and bodily faculties. Still, just now that he was away, I almost felt mother-sick, and I decided to write a long and affectionate letter to her as soon as I got home.

Meanwhile I walked on haphazardly. After wandering about for an hour, I found myself unexpectedly before Teleny's house. I had wended my steps thitherwards, without knowing where I went. I looked up at Teleny's windows with longing eyes. How I loved that house. I could have kissed the very stones on which he had stepped.

The night was dark but clear, the street—a very quiet one—was not of the best lighted, and for some reason or other the nearest gas-lamp had gone out.

As I kept staring up at the windows, it seemed as if I saw a faint light glimmering through the crevices of the shut-up blinds. 'Of course,' I thought, "it is only my imagination.'

I strained my eyes. 'No, surely, I am not mistaken,' I said, audibly to myself, 'surely there is a light.'

Had Teleny come back?

Perhaps he had been seized with the same

state of dejection which had come over me when we parted. The anquish visible on my ghastly face must have paralyzed him, and in the state which he was he could not play, so he had come back. Perhaps, also, the concert had been postponed.

Perhaps it was thieves?

But if Teleny—?

No, the very idea was absurd. How could I suspect the man I loved of infidelity. I shrank from such a supposition as from something heinous—from a kind of moral pollution. No, it must be anything else but that. The key of the door downstairs was in my hand, I was already in the house.

I crept stealthily upstairs, in the dark, thinking of the first night I had accompanied my friend there, thinking how we had stopped to kiss and hug each other at every step.

But now, without my friend, the darkness was weighing upon me, overpowering, crushing me. I was at last on the landing of the *entresol* where my friend lived; the whole house was perfectly quiet.

Before putting in the key, I looked through the hole. Had Teleny, or his servant, left the gas lighted in the antechamber and in one of the rooms?

Then the remembrance of the broken mirror came into my mind; all kinds of horrible thoughts flitted through my brain. Then, again, in spite of myself, the awful apprehension of having been supplanted in Teleny's affection by someone else forced itself upon me.

No, it was too ridiculous. Who could this rival be?

Like a thief I introduced the key in the lock; the hinges were well oiled, the door yielded noiselessly, and opened. I shut it carefully, without its emitting the slightest sound. I stole in on tiptoe.

There were thick carpets everywhere that muffled my steps. I went to the room where, a few hours before, I had known such rapturous bliss.

It was lighted.

I heard stifled sounds within.

I knew but too well what those sounds meant. For the first time I felt the shattering pangs of jealousy. It seemed as if a poisoned dagger had all at once been thrust into my heart; as if an enormous hydra had caught my body between its jaws, and had driven its huge fangs through the flesh of my chest.

Why had I come here? What was I to do now? Where was I to go?

I felt as if I were collapsing.

My hand was already on the door, but before opening it I did what I suppose most people would have done. Trembling from head to foot, sick at heart, I bent down and looked through the keyhole.

Was I dreaming—was this a dreadful nightmare?

I stuck my nails deep into my flesh to convince myself of my self-consciousness.

And yet I could not feel sure that I was alive and awake.

Life at times loses its sense of reality; it appears to us like a weird, optical illusion—a phantasmagoric bubble that will disappear at the slightest breath.

I held my breath, and looked.

This was, then, no illusion—no vision of my overheated fancy.

There, on that chair—warm yet with our embraces—two beings were seated.

But who were they?

Perhaps Teleny had ceded his apartment to some friend for that night. Perhaps he had forgotten to mention the fact to me, or else he had not thought it necessary to do so.

Yes, surely, it must be so. Teleny could not deceive me.

I looked again. The light within the room being much brighter than that of the hall, I was able to perceive everything clearly.

A man whose form I could not see was seated on that chair contrived by Teleny's ingenious mind to enhance sensual bliss. A woman with dark, dishevelled hair, robed in a white satin gown, was sitting astride him. Her back was thus turned to the door.

I strained my eyes to catch every detail, and I saw that she was not really seated but standing on tiptoe, so that, though rather stout, she skipped lightly upon the man's knees.

Though I could not see, I understood that every time she fell she received within her hole the good-sized pivot on which she seemed so tightly wedged. Moreover, that the pleasure she received thereby was so thrilling that it caused her to rebound like an elastic ball, but only to fall again, and thus engulf within her pulpy, spongy, well-moistened lips, the whole of that quivering rod of pleasure down to its hairy root. Whoever she was—grand lady or whore —she was no tyro, but a woman of great experience, to be able to ride that Cytherean race with such consummate skill.

As I gazed on, I saw that her enjoyment kept getting stronger and ever stronger: it was reaching its paroxysm. From an amble she had gone on quietly to a trot, then to a canter; then, as she rode along, she clasped, with ever-increasing passion, the head of the man on whose knees she was astride. It was clear that the contact of her lover's lips and the swelling and wriggling of his tool within her, thrilled her to an erotic rage, so she went off in a gallop, thus—

Leaping higher, higher, higher,
With a desperate desire

to reach the delightful aim of her journey.

In the meanwhile, the male, whoever he was, after having passed his hands on the massy lobes of her hindparts, began to pat and press and knead her breasts, adding thus to her pleasure a thousand little caresses which almost maddened her.

I remember now a most curious fact, showing the way in which our brains work, and how our mind is attracted by slight extraneous objects, even when engrossed by the saddest thoughts. I remember feeling a certain artistic pleasure at the ever-changing effect of light and shadow thrown on different parts of the lady's rich satin gown, as it kept shimmering under the rays of the lamp hanging overhead. I recollect admiring its pearly, silky, metallic tints, now glistening, then glimmering or fading into a dull lustre.

Just then, however, the train of her gown had got entangled somewhere round the leg of the chair, so, as this incident impeded her rhythmical and ever quicker movements, enclasping her lover's neck, she managed deftly to cast off her gown, and thus remained stark naked in the man's embrace.

What a splendid body she had! Juno's in all its majesty could not have been more perfect. I had, however, hardly time to admire her luxuriant beauty, her grace, her strength, the splendid symmetry of her outlines, her agility, or her skill, for the race was now reaching its end.

They were both trembling under the spell of that rapturous titillation which just precedes the overflowing of the spermatic ducts. Evidently the tip of the man's tool was being sucked by the mouth of the vagina, a contraction of all the nerves had ensued; the sheath in which the whole column was enclosed had tightened, and both their bodies were writhing convulsively.

Surely after such overpowering spasms, prolapsus and inflammation of the womb must ensue, but then what rapture she must give.

Then I heard mingled sighs and panting, low cooings, gurgling sounds of lust, dying in stifled kisses given by lips that still cleaved languidly to each other; then, as they quivered with the last pangs of pleasure, I quivered in agony, for I was almost sure that that man must be my lover.

'But who can that hateful woman be?' I asked myself.

Still, the sight of those two naked bodies clasped in such a thrilling embrace, those two massy lobes of flesh, as white as newly-fallen snow; the smothered sound of their ecstatic bliss, overcame for a moment my excruciating jealousy, and I could hardly forbear from rushing into the room. My fluttering bird—my nightingale, as they call it in Italy—like Sterne's starling—was trying to escape from its cage; and not only that, but it also lifted up its head in such a way that it seemed to wish to reach the keyhole.

My fingers were already on the handle of the door. Why should I not burst in and have my share in the feast, though in a humbler way, and like a beggar go in by the back entrance?

Why not, indeed!

Just then, the lady whose arms were still tightly clasped round the man's neck, said,—

'Bon Dieu! how good it is! I have not felt such intensity of rapture for a long time.'

For an instant I was stunned. My fingers relinquished the handle of the door, my arm fell, even my bird drooped down, lifeless.

What a voice!

'But I know that voice,' I said to myself. 'Its sound is most familiar to me. Only the blood which is reaching up to my head and tingling in my ears prevents me from understanding whose voice it is.'

While in my amazement I had lifted up my head, she had got up and turned round. Standing as she was now, and nearer the door, my eyes could not reach her face, still I could see her naked body—from the shoulders downwards. It was a marvelous figure, the finest one I had ever seen. A woman's torso in the height of its beauty.

Her skin was of a dazzling whiteness, and could vie in smoothness as well as in pearly lustre with the satin of the gown she had cast off. Her breasts—perhaps a little too big to be aesthetically beautiful—seemed to belong to one of those voluptuous Venetian courtesans painted by Titian; they stood out plump and hard as if swollen with milk; the protruding nipples, like two dainty pink buds, were surrounded by a fringe of the passion flower.

The powerful line of the hips showed to advantage the beauty of the legs. Her stomach—so perfectly round and smooth—was half covered with a magnificent fur, as black and as glossy as a beaver's, and yet I could see that she had been a mother, for it was *moire* like watered silk. From the yawning, humid lips pearly drops were slowly trickling down.

Though not exactly in early youth, she was no less desirable for all that. Her beauty had all the gorgeousness of the full-blown rose, and the pleasure she evidently could give was that of the incarnadined flower in its fragrant bloom; that bliss which makes the bee which sucks its honey swoon in its bosom with delight. That aphrodisiacal body, as I could see, was made for, and surely had afforded pleasure to, more than one man, inasmuch as she had evidently been formed by nature to be one of Venus' Votaresses.

After thus exhibiting her wonderful beauty to my dazed eyes, she stepped aside and I could see the partner of her dalliance. Though his face was covered with his hands, it was Teleny. There was no mistake about it.

First his god-like figure, then his phallus, which I knew so well, then—I almost fainted as my eyes fell upon it—on his finger glittered the ring I had given him.

She spoke again.

He drew his hands from off his face.

It was he! It was Teleny—my friend—my lover—my life!

How can I describe what I felt? It seemed to me as if I were breathing fire; as if a rain of glowing ashes were being poured down upon me.

The door was locked. I caught its handle, and shook it as a mighty whirlwind shakes the sails of some large frigate, and then tears them to shreds. I burst it open.

I staggered on the sill. The floor seemed to be giving way under my feet; everything was spinning around me; I was in the very midst of a mighty whirlpool. I caught myself by the doorposts not to fall, for there, to my inexpressible horror, I found myself face to face with—my own mother!

There was a threefold cry of shame, of terror,

of despair—a piercing, shrill cry that rang through the still night air, awakening all the inmates of that quiet house from their peaceful slumbers.

— And you—what did you do?

— What did I do? I really don't know. I must have said something—I must have done something, but I have not the slightest recollection of what it was. Then I stumbled downstairs in the dark. It was like going down, down into a deep well. I only remember running through the gloomy streets—running like a madman, whither I knew not.

I felt cursed like Cain, or like the Eternal Wanderer, so I ran on at random.

I had fled from them, would that I had been able to flee from myself likewise.

All at once, at the corner of the street, I ran against someone. We both recoiled from each other. I aghast and terror-stricken; he, simply, astonished.

— And whom did you meet?

— My own image. A man exactly like myself —my *Doppelganger*, in fact. He stared at me for an instant, and then passed on. I, instead, ran with whatever strength was left in me.

My head was reeling, my strength was breaking down, I stumbled several times, still I ran on.

Was I mad?

All at once, panting, breathless, bruised in body and in mind, I found myself standing on the bridge—nay, on the very same spot on which I had stood some months before.

I uttered a harsh, jarring laugh that frightened me. So it had come to this, after all.

I cast a hurried glance around me. A dark shadow loomed in the distance. Was it my other self?

Trembling, shuddering, maddened, without a moment's thought, I climbed on the parapet and plunged head foremost into the foaming flood beneath.

I was again in the very midst of a whirlpool, I heard the noise of rushing waters in my ears; darkness was pressing closely round me, a world of thoughts flitted through my brain with astonishing rapidity, and then, for some time, nothing more.

Only I vaguely remember opening my eyes, and seeing as in a looking glass my own ghastly face staring at me.

A blank came over me again. When at last I recovered my senses I found myself in the *Morgue*—that dreadful charnel house, the *Morgue!* They had believed me dead, and had carried me there.

I looked around me, I saw nothing but unknown faces. My other self was nowhere to be seen.

— But did he really exist?

— He did.

— And who was he?

— A man of my own age, and so exactly like myself that we might have been taken for twin brothers.

— And he had saved your life?

— Yes; it appears that on meeting me, he was not only struck with the strong likeness that existed between us, but also by the wildness of my appearance, therefore he was prompted to follow me. Having seen me throw myself into the water, he ran after me and managed to get me out.

— And did you see him again?

— I did, poor fellow! But that is another strange incident of my too-eventful life. Perhaps I'll tell it to you some other time.

— Then from the *Morgue?*

— I begged to be transported to some neighboring hospital, where I could have a private room all to myself, where I should see nobody, where nobody would see me; for I felt ill—very ill.

As I was about to enter the carriage and go off from the charnel house, a shrouded corpse was borne thither. They said it was a young man who had just committed suicide.

I shuddered with fear, a terrible suspicion came into my mind. I begged the doctor who was with me to bid the coachman stop. I must see that corpse. It must be Teleny. The physician did not heed me, and the cab drove on.

On reaching the hospital, my attendant seeing my state of mind sent to inquire who the dead man was. The name they mentioned was unknown to me.

Three days passed. When I say three days, I mean a weary, endless space of time. The opiates the doctor had given me had put me to sleep, and had even stopped the horrible quivering of my nerves. But what opiate can cure a crushed heart?

At the end of those three days my manager had found me out, and came to see me. He seemed terrified with my appearance.

Poor fellow! he was at a loss what to say. He avoided anything that might jar upon my nerves, so he spoke about business. I listened for a while, though his words had no meaning for me, then I managed to find out from him that my mother had left town, and that she had already written to him from Geneva, where she was at present staying. He did not mention Teleny's name and I myself durst not utter it.

He offered me a room in his house, but I refused, and drove home with him. Now that my mother had gone I was obliged to go there—at least for a few days.

No one had called during my absence; there was no letter or message left for me, so that I too could say:

'My kinsfolk have failed, and my familiar friends have forgotten me.

'They that dwell in mine house, and my maids, count me for a stranger: I am an alien in their sight.'

Like Job I felt now that—

'All my inward friends abhorred me: and they whom I loved are turned against me.

'Yea, young children despised me.'

Still I was anxious to know something about Teleny, for terrors made me afraid on every side. Had he gone off with my mother, and not left the slightest message for me?

Still, what was he to write?

If he had remained in town, had I not told

him that, whatever his fault might be, I should always forgive him if he sent me back the ring.

— And had he sent it back, could you have pardoned him?

— I loved him.

I could not bear this state of things any longer. Truth, however painful, was preferable to this dreadful suspense.

I called on Briancourt. I found his studio shut. I went to his house. He had not been at home for two days. The servants did not know where he was. They thought that he had, perhaps, gone to his father's in Italy.

Disconsolate, I roamed about the streets, and soon I found myself again before Teleny's house. The door downstairs was still open. I stole by the porter's lodge, frightened lest I might be stopped and told that my friend was not at home. No one, however, noticed me. I crept upstairs, shivering, nerveless, sick. I put the key in the lock, the door yielded noiselessly as it had done a few nights before. I went in.

Then I asked myself what I was to do next, and I almost turned on my heels and ran off.

As I stood there wavering, I thought I heard a faint moan.

I listened. All was quiet.

No, there was a groan—a low, dying wail.

It seemed to proceed from the white room.

I shuddered with horror.

I rushed in.

The recollection of what I saw freezes the very marrow in my bones.

'Even when I remember I am afraid, and trembling taketh hold of my flesh.'

I saw a pool of coagulated blood on the dazzling-white, fur carpet, and Teleny, half-fallen on the bearskin-covered couch. A small dagger was plunged in his breast, and the blood continued to trickle out of the wound.

I threw myself upon him; he was not quite dead; he groaned; he opened his eyes.

Overwhelmed by grief, distracted by terror, I lost all presence of mind. I let go of his head, and clasped my throbbing temples between my palms, trying to collect my thoughts and to dominate myself so as to help my friend.

Should I pluck the knife from the wound? No, it might be fatal.

Oh, if I had a slight knowledge of surgery! But having none, the only thing I could do was to call for help.

I ran onto the landing; I screamed out with all my might:

'Help, help! Fire, fire! Help!'

On the stairs my voice sounded like thunder.

The porter was out of his lodge in an instant.

I heard doors and windows opening. I again screamed out, 'Help!' and then, snatching up a bottle of cognac from the dining room sideboard, I hurried back to my friend.

I moistened his lips; I poured a few spoonfuls of brandy, drop by drop, down his mouth.

Teleny opened his eyes again. They were veiled and almost dead; only that mournful look he always had, had increased to such intensity that his pupils were as gloomy as a yawning grave; they thrilled me with an unutterable anguish. I could hardly stand that pitiful, stony look; I felt my nerves stiffen; my breath stopped; I burst out into a convulsive sobbing.

'Oh, Teleny! why did you kill yourself?' I moaned. 'Could you have doubted my forgiveness, my love?'

He evidently heard me, and tried to speak, but I could not catch the slightest sound.

'No, you must not die, I cannot part with you, you are my very life.'

I felt my fingers pressed slightly, imperceptibly.

The porter now made his appearance, but he stopped on the threshold, frightened, terrified.

'A doctor—for mercy's sake, a doctor! Take a carriage—run!' I said, imploringly.

Other people began to come in. I waved them back.

'Shut the door. Let no one else enter, but for God's sake fetch a doctor before it is too late!'

The people, aghast, stood at a distance, staring at the dreadful sight.

Teleny again moved his lips.

'Hush! silence!' I whispered sternly. 'He speaks!'

I felt racked at not being able to understand a single word of what he wanted to say. After several fruitless attempts I managed to make out:

'Forgive!'

'If I forgive you, my angel? But I not only forgive you, I'd give my life for you!'

The dreary expression of his eyes had deepened, still, grievous as they were, a happier look was to be seen in them. Little by little the heartfelt sadness teemed with ineffable sweetness. I could hardly bear his glances any longer; they were torturing me. Their burning fire sank far into my soul.

Then he again uttered a whole phrase, the only two words of which I guessed rather than heard were—

'Briancourt—letter.'

After that his waning strength began to forsake him.

As I looked at him I saw that his eyes were getting clouded, a faint film came over them, he did not seem to see me any more. Yes, they were getting ever more glazed and glassy.

He did not attempt to speak, his lips were tightly shut. Still, after a few moments, he opened his mouth spasmodically; he gasped. He uttered a low, choking raucous sound.

It was his last breath. Death's awful rattle.

The room was hushed.

I saw the people cross themselves. Some women knelt, and began to mumble prayers.

A horrible light dawned upon me.

What! He is dead, then?

His head fell lifeless on my chest.

I uttered a shrill cry. I called for help.

A doctor had come at last.

'He is beyond help,' the doctor said; 'he is dead.'

What! My Teleny dead?

I looked around at the people. Aghast, they

seemed to shrink from me. The room began to spin around. I knew nothing more. I had fainted.

I only came back to my senses after some weeks. A certain dullness had come over me, and the

> *Earth seemed a desert*
> *I was bound to traverse.*

Still the idea of self-murder never returned to my mind. Death did not seem to want me.

In the meanwhile, my story, in veiled words, had appeared in every newspaper. It was too dainty a bit of gossip not to spread about at once like wildfire.

Even the letter Teleny had written to me before his suicide—stating that his debts, which had been paid by my mother, had been the cause of his infidelity—had got to be public property.

Then, Heaven having revealed my iniquity, the earth rose against me; for if Society does not ask you to be intrinsically good, it asks you to make a goodly show of morality, and, above all, to avoid scandals. Therefore a famous clergyman—a saintly man—preached at that time an edifying sermon, which began with the following text:

'His remembrance shall perish from the earth, and he shall have no name in the street.'

And he ended it, saying:

'He shall be driven from light into darkness, and chased out of the world.'

Whereupon all Teleny's friends, the Zophars, the Eliphazes, and the Bildads uttered a loud Amen!

— And Briancourt and your mother?

— Oh, I promised to tell you her adventures! I may do so some other time. They are well worth hearing.

THE END

*Non-fiction   **The Incest Chronicles of the Loring Family

Ship To:_____

Address:_____

City, State, Zip:_____

I am over 21:   ☐   Total Remittance Enclosed: $_____

REGENT HOUSE (BOOK DIVISION)
Box 9506, North Hollywood, California 91605